MEMORY
MAZE

Look for more action and humor from

GORDON KORMAN

The Hypnotists

The Swindle series

Swindle

Zoobreak

Framed

Showoff

Hideout

Jackpot

Unleashed

The Titanic trilogy

The Kidnapped trilogy

The On the Run series

The Dive trilogy

The Everest trilogy

The Island trilogy

Radio Fifth Grade

The Toilet Paper Tigers

The Chicken Doesn't Skate

This Can't Be Happening at Macdonald Hall!

MEMORY MAZE

BOOK TWO OF THE HYPNOTISTS

SCHOLASTIC INC.

FOR SHARI AND JEFFREY

This book was originally published in hardcover by Scholastic Press in 2014.

ISBN 978-0-545-50332-7

12 11 10 9 8 7 6 5 4 3 2 1 15 16 17 18 19 20/0

Printed in the U.S.A. 40
First printing 2015

The text type was set in Adobe Garamond.
Book design by Nina Goffi

PROLOGUE

The doorman hadn't seen another human being for two solid hours when the stretch limousine whispered up to the curb. Visitors were uncommon at four in the morning, even in New York City. Three tall figures got out of the back, their faces shadowed by the upturned collars of their jackets.

"It's a no-parking zone," the doorman told them, but got no answer. "What can I do for you gentlemen?"

In reply, the tallest of the three stepped directly in front of him, his features suddenly illuminated in the streetlight — a hawk nose, striking brows, and piercing black eyes. His name was Dr. Elias Mako.

"You are very calm and relaxed," he said in a mellow tone.

Entranced by Mako's mesmerizing gaze, the doorman was surprised to note that, yes, he *was* calm, and so relaxed that he had to recline against the pole that held up the awning. What a pleasant feeling! Normally, a building-security employee should be suspicious of newcomers at this hour. But not these three. He couldn't quite put his finger on what their business here might be, but he was sure it was necessary.

"You will go behind the desk, and you will hand over the superintendent's key to apartment 7J," Mako went on. "You will remember nothing of us, or this conversation."

The doorman did as he was told, absurdly happy to be of service to these fine people.

Mako and his companions rode the elevator to the seventh floor and moved silently along the carpeted corridor to the apartment they sought.

"Remember," Mako cautioned, "your job is to take care of the mother and father. Leave the boy to me."

"I'm not afraid of Jackson Dopus!" muttered Wilson DeVries, who, at fifteen years old, was nearly as tall as Mako.

"You should be," Mako replied, casting a cold grimace on his student. "We all should be. Jackson Opus is the nexus of the two greatest bloodlines in hypnotic history. And his power grows stronger every day. He alone can stand in the way of our plans."

"That's what we're here for," put in DeRon Marcus, the third member of the team. He too was a pupil of Mako's at the Sentia Institute. "They won't know what hit them."

Mako frowned. "A little less bragging, please. I would never take the extraordinary step we're about to take if it weren't absolutely necessary." He slipped the key in the lock and opened the door.

Even by the dim light coming in from the hallway, it was apparent that the apartment was empty. No furniture, no window dressings, no people.

Mako was shocked, but his tone remained even. "This is . . . disappointing."

Wilson cursed under his breath. "The gutless wonder took off!"

DeRon's confidence melted away. "What happens now?"

Sentia's founder and director walked slowly around the perimeter of the living room, as if searching for an explanation from the bare walls. "Where are you, Jackson Opus?"

The walls had no reply.

Mako knew he would find the answer sooner or later — even if it meant doing some damage in the process.

The blade sang by Jax's ear and grazed the padding on his shoulder. Another quarter inch and it would have taken his head off. He gritted his teeth and parried the next blow, then lashed out with his own weapon, going for a stab at the chest. But his opponent was too quick for him. He danced away, and came back strong.

The next thing Jax knew, the sword was slicing straight for his throat, and he felt the end was near. At the last second, he flailed blindly with his own weapon. There was a clash of metal on metal, and somehow the thrust was swept aside. But the battle was not going well. That was plain. Sensing the tide turning, his adversary pressed his advantage, growing more aggressive with every move. Jax fought back with all his skill but still found himself backing up, giving ground, his breath heaving in his chest, sweat stinging his eyes.

When his back bumped up against the wall, there was nowhere else to retreat.

The game was up.

"Okay, okay!" he gasped. "I give!"

But the enemy was unwilling to leave it at that. One

final thrust, and Jax felt the end of the foil pressing against his stomach. Angrily, he flipped up his fencing mask and barked, "Really, man? Back off!"

Too late, he saw the fleeting vision of himself standing there in full fencing gear, mask raised. It was like a picture-in-picture image from a TV, and Jax knew better than anyone what it signified. No sword could match the power of Jackson Opus's remarkable eyes. By flipping up his mask and glaring at Gary Northrop, he had accidentally hypnotized the boy.

Just a few months before, Jax would have had no idea what he was seeing. It had taken Dr. Elias Mako and his Sentia Institute to explain it to him. A mesmeric link had formed between Jax and Gary. In a way, part of Jax was inside his opponent's head, peering at himself through Gary's eyes.

Still masked and in full gear, Gary began to reverse across the gym, heading for the exit, heels first.

"What are you doing?" Jax asked in bewilderment as his opponent passed between other fencers, almost getting skewered a couple of times. He kept on going, right through the half-court basketball game on the other side of the gym.

Then Jax remembered. His exact words had been *Back off.* To a subject under hypnotic control, that was nothing less than a specific instruction. Gary was backing off.

"It's okay, man, I didn't mean it!" But by this time, the subject was lost in the shouts of the game and the percussion of the basketball on the hardwood floor. He retreated, straight out the door of the gym, a bounce pass twanging his foil as he shuffled by.

Jax started after him, pulling down his mask as he ran. No sense looking at the guy again. All subjects were different, but it was obvious that Gary was easily "bent." Much of the science of hypnotism was unknown, even by Dr. Mako, who was the world's foremost authority on the subject. How long would Gary keep going? Who knew? He wasn't going to backpedal around the world, but the effect might not wear off until he found himself out in traffic somewhere.

Anything that happened to the guy would be 100 percent Jax's fault.

He caught up with Gary, who was half-buried in the flower bed on the front lawn of Haywood Middle School. He'd fallen over a plaster garden gnome and was thrashing around, still trying to back up. His white fencing uniform was caked with damp black soil.

Jax rushed over and helped him to his feet. It was only recently that he'd discovered he was a mind-bender. He was just learning to control the effects of his powers.

"It's okay, Gary," he said. "You can stop now."

But Gary was deep in his trance, kicking up dirt as he scrambled to withdraw.

With a sigh, Jax flipped his mask up again, and also Gary's, to make sure there was eye contact. Jax had the old Opus family trait of eyes that changed color, ranging from pale green to deep purple. At that moment, he was passing from charcoal gray into royal blue. Obviously, he wasn't going to get away with a shortcut here. In order to release Gary from the last command, he would have to be re-hypnotized, this time by the book.

"You will stop backing off," he said when the PIP image reappeared. Gary's struggles ceased abruptly. "When I count to three, you'll wake up in a happy and relaxed mood. You'll remember nothing about this — especially the part with me in it. Oh, yeah — and there's a worm on your shoulder. Go get yourself cleaned up. One, two, three."

Gary popped up and disappeared inside the school, leaving a trail of black earth and mashed chrysanthemums behind.

Jax exhaled in relief. The last thing he needed was for the Haywood staff to think that Jackson Opus was the cause of anything peculiar. That was the whole reason he'd dragged his parents to this Connecticut town, seventy-seven miles away from everything they knew and cared about in New York City. It was also why he was no longer Jackson Opus. Here in Haywood, he went by the name Jack Magnus. It was all part of an elaborate story — one that had turned his life and the lives of his family upside down. This was the hypnotist's version of the Witness Protection Program. They were hiding out here — hiding from the evil intentions of Dr. Elias Mako.

Jax had started out as the Sentia Institute's brightest star — but all that had turned sour when he'd refused to go along with Mako's plan to use mass hypnotism to rig a presidential election. The director didn't like to be told no.

In fact, he'd tried to murder Jax's parents and had very nearly succeeded in killing Jax as well.

A mesmeric homicide attempt left no evidence, so there was no way to go to the police. A hypnotist was always armed with an invisible weapon. You could be defeated before you guessed that you were in a fight. Police could provide zero protection from such a threat. They probably couldn't be persuaded that the danger even existed.

The Opuses' only solution had been to vanish.

In the gym, Coach Riley regarded the returning Jax disapprovingly. "Gotta work harder, Magnus. Northrop was all over you. Your stamina has to improve if you want to make this team."

"I will, Coach." Jax promised. He had very little interest in fencing. He'd only chosen the sport because he'd have to wear the mask. Anything to keep his treacherous multicolored eyes from doing any damage.

And I couldn't even get that right, he told himself bitterly.

He cast an envious glance at the basketball game. *That* was his sport, and he was pretty good at it, too. But he'd played back in New York. Dr. Mako would know that. And while no one could monitor every seventh-grade basketball game in the country, it never paid to underestimate Dr. Mako.

The locker room was a scene of raucous towel-snapping and laughter as the team made fun of the hapless Gary, who was still shaking soil out of his hair.

"I don't know how it happened," he said for the umpteenth time. He turned his attention to Jax. "You were there, Jack! How did I end up in the mud?"

Jax shrugged. "Beats me. You just went. I figured you needed some air or something."

Gary clung to this theory like a drowning man. "I needed some air, so chill out!"

That was one of the things Jax had learned when Dr. Mako had been his mentor, not his mortal enemy: After a hypnotic experience, most subjects filled in the blanks in their memories naturally enough. It was a lot easier than wrapping their minds around the idea that something truly paranormal had taken place.

As soon as Jax's fencing mask came off, a pair of dark sunglasses went on. He wore these all day, even in class. It was a sore point with the Haywood faculty, who suspected that he was either arrogant or asleep behind those shades. The real reason, of course, was to keep his ever-changing eyes and their power away from innocent bystanders. His homeroom teacher, Mr. Isaacs, called him the movie star, and it was definitely not a compliment. If his fellow students thought he was a conceited jerk, well, then so be it. It was better than the whole school backing up into a mud bog, like Gary. Jax was here to hide, not to be elected Mr. Popularity. And, anyway, no one in this one-horse town could ever be a best friend like Tommy Cicerelli, whom he'd left behind in New York. He'd had to cut all ties with the guy, for safety's sake, and Tommy's own protection.

Of all the miserable things he'd had to do because of Elias Mako, that one was still the toughest.

Every time Jax approached their two-bedroom rental home on Gardenia Street, the calamity that had befallen the Opuses was laid out before him like a bad dream. It was a long way from their luxury doorman apartment building to this ramshackle house, with its sagging shutters, peeling paint, and missing roof tiles. When the rain blew in from the west, the family had to organize a bucket brigade. The plumbing was in constant conversation with the radiators, and the walls and floors hadn't been painted and refinished since General Eisenhower was a cadet.

Inside, Mrs. Opus — now Mrs. Magnus — sat in the dingy living room, holding her head as if it were about to fall off and roll across the threadbare carpet.

"What's wrong, Mom? Another migraine?"

In answer, she gestured straight up with her thumb. From above came a long, loud bubbling noise that vibrated through the entire house.

"Axel's just gargling," Jax tried to explain. "He says there's a lot of mold in the attic, so he's trying to keep his throat clear."

"It sounds like someone's strangling him up there,"

she said, near tears. "I swear, one of these days it's going to be me!"

The gurgling ended in a cascade of spitting, which was followed by a crisp, *"Ahhhhh!"*

"Mom . . ." Jax was reproachful. "He saved your life. He saved all our lives. And he moved into the attic because he's trying to help us now."

"I know," she said, abashed. "But why can't he do it from a decent distance? You're not home for his morning exercises! He shakes his feet — his ankles must be made of rubber!" Mrs. Opus was actually Dr. Opus, a chiropractor with a bustling New York practice. She'd been forced to abandon that in favor of a position as a bookkeeper for a local bakery. "No one should have to live like this."

"We've been through this a million times," her son explained patiently. "When it comes to hypnotism, he's the one person who can stand up to Mako. And he can help me develop my skills to the point where I can do it, too. I know it's hard with him living in the attic. But if we're ever going to get our lives back, this is the way it has to be."

Heavy, creaking footfalls could be heard on the stairs. Mrs. Opus cringed with each one. And then he was with them in the living room — a slight, sixty-something-year-old man with long gray hair pulled back into a ponytail. He smelled of mouthwash and mothballs. His face was lined, but his expression was open and friendly. There was an almost childlike playfulness about him. In fact, he was a brilliant man, a powerful mind-bender on a par with Dr. Mako himself.

His name was Axel Braintree, and he was the founder of the Sandman's Guild, an association of fellow hypnotists that was about as different from the Sentia Institute as it was possible to be.

"Ah, Jax — I trust you learned things in school today."

Jax reflected on his fencing experience. He'd definitely learned when not to flip up his mask. "You might say that."

There was a key in the lock, and the door opened to admit Jax's father. Trading his career as the manager of a Manhattan Bentley dealership for a lowest-man-on-the-totem-pole job selling used cars had been a crushing blow for Ashton Opus. Today, though, there was a spring in his step, and he was all smiles.

"I sold that Chevy Silverado today," he announced proudly. "You remember the buyer, Jax — you went with us on the test-drive. Well, today he signed on the dotted line."

"Gee, that's great, Dad." Jax tried to sound enthusiastic, yet under Braintree's accusing eye, he found it hard. He kept his mouth shut — no way was he going to deprive his father of the triumph of his first sale in the new job.

After dinner, Jax was loading the dishwasher when Braintree cornered him in the kitchen. "You went along for the test-drive?" he probed. "Are you sure that's all you did?"

Jax shrugged his innocence. "It was three days ago."

"That's not the meat of the coconut," the old man persisted.

Jax relented. There was no sense fighting him. Braintree knew everything. He was spooky that way.

"Okay, okay, I bent the guy. I implanted a post-hypnotic suggestion that he had to have the Silverado. I set up a forty-eight-hour trigger before it kicked in so it wouldn't look suspicious." Jax spread his hands in a pleading gesture. "What's the harm in helping out my dad after all the misery I've put him through?"

"No harm at all," Braintree agreed gravely, "except maybe to the man who might have been looking for a Mini Cooper and drove out with a giant pickup."

Jax flushed, and his eyes darkened two shades of blue. He'd thought only of boosting his father's confidence. He hadn't considered the buyer at all, beyond the fact that he needed a vehicle and now he had one.

Braintree always assumed a grandfatherly air when he was about to preach. "Hypnotism is not hard for a sandman. It comes naturally to us. What *is* hard is resisting the temptation to use our power to make life easier for ourselves. Each morning you wake up, and everything you could possibly want is within your grasp. Can't afford that flat-screen TV? You can bend the salesperson into lowering the price. A nickel sounds reasonable. Or you could pay full price. You just have to stop at the bank, where a mesmerized teller will let you withdraw the money from an account you don't have. Failed that math test? A little eye contact with the teacher — that's not an F; that's an A. Need a date for the sock hop? How about the head cheerleader? She doesn't know it yet, but she really likes you."

"What's a sock hop? How old *are* you, Axel?"

"You see my point, though?"

"Yeah, I get it," Jax conceded. "You're not talking to your Sandman's Guild here."

"That's exactly who I'm talking to," the old man returned. "You just proved that. If you use your ability for personal advantage — even if it's just to move up three places in line at a movie theater — it's no different than Elias Mako trying to steal a presidential election."

Jax flinched. Being compared to Mako really hurt.

"In the Sandman's Guild," Braintree went on, "we talk these things out, and help each other resist the impulse to take hypnotic shortcuts."

"I've watched your sandmen work a crowd," Jax retorted. "I've never seen so much pickpocketing in my life. I think some of those people are missing gold teeth."

The old man nodded. "Admitted. They fall off the wagon sometimes. Nobody's perfect, as you've just demonstrated. And sometimes we're forced to use our powers for the common good — like when you used yours to thwart Mako's plans. Let's not forget how the guild members aided you and your family when you had to disappear from Manhattan."

Jax bit his tongue. Braintree's sandmen had come through in a huge way when it had been time for the Opuses to lam it from New York. They had packed up the entire apartment, bending neighbors and doormen so they'd forget the family had ever existed. Mass hypnotisms had been staged at city hall, the passport office, and the Department of Motor Vehicles to come up with the documents to create the Magnuses of Haywood and make the Opuses of Manhattan wink out of existence. According to city records, Mrs. Opus's chiropractic clinic had been shut down due to a bedbug infestation. No one at the Bentley dealership remembered anyone named Ashton Opus, and there was no record of him having ever worked there. The files at I.S. 222 clearly showed that Jax's former ID number belonged to an exchange student who had since returned to a small African nation that was not on any map. It was the one thing that could bring a smile to Jax's lips these days — the thought of Dr. Mako trying to track Jax down at school, only to find he was inquiring about Mwango Gbuzi. Tommy would have gotten a real kick out of that one — except that Tommy himself had been bent. To him, Jackson Opus was barely a memory.

Even now, the sandmen were keeping an eye on Dr. Mako and the Sentia Institute, and reporting back to Braintree. Mako may have been the most dangerous mind-bender on the planet, but he was up against a collection of con artists, tricksters, embezzlers, and petty thieves.

"It's a little confusing, you know," Jax complained. "First you tell me it's bad to use hypnotism. Then you say the whole reason you're here is to teach me how to strengthen my ability. Which is it going to be?"

"You are descended from the two greatest families in mesmeric history," the old man explained patiently. "That's hard to see, since neither of your parents have the talent. It all came to you. We can only guess how powerful you may become. Mako knows this, and he must suspect that eventually your strength will surpass his. He tried to recruit you, and that didn't work out. Now his only option is to destroy you while he still can."

Jax was unconvinced. "Every time I tried to bend Mako, he wiped the floor with me."

"The sandman's power is like a muscle," Braintree lectured. "Even Mr. Universe doesn't start with the heaviest barbells on day one. That's why I'm here — to pump you up. Somebody has to stop Mako, and you have the potential to be that somebody."

"What about you?"

The old man shook his head. "I might be able to approach him in skill, yet not in ambition and ruthlessness. To match him, I'd have to risk becoming something just as bad. But you — you will one day make meat loaf out of us both."

"Yeah?" challenged Jax. "When?"

In answer, the founder of the Sandman's Guild turned his full gaze to Jax's multicolored eyes. Jax was instantly aware of an odd sensation, the mental equivalent of swallowing water down the wrong pipe. Braintree was trying to hypnotize him — and inviting him to fight back.

There was nothing kind and open about the old man's expression now. His intensity was scary, his focus arrow-straight. Jax felt the familiar stirring in his brain that indicated his mind was being probed. In an enormous rush of willpower, he muscled the incursion out of his head, staring at Braintree with irises deepening to purple.

Jax pressed his advantage, his eyes boring into Braintree's skull. He could see the beginnings of the PIP image attempting to establish itself in his field of vision. He was winning this battle.

I'm doing it! I'm taking down Axel Braintree! he told himself exultantly.

The momentary lapse in concentration cost him the upper hand. Braintree repelled the attack with a wave of energy that felt like a depth charge going off in Jax's mind. Jax staggered back a half step, and in that instant the old man looked away, breaking the connection. The PIP image popped and vanished.

"You see?" Braintree's voice was weak but satisfied. "You're packing a cannon between those ears. You're the real McTavish."

"So how come I couldn't seal the deal?" Jax panted, exhausted.

The old man shrugged. "I'm a street fighter. But you're going to be the heavyweight champ."

3

At the corner of Thirty-Fourth Street and Seventh Avenue, business was lousy for Evelyn Lolis. Standing an even six feet tall in flats, she normally attracted attention. But today no one seemed interested in seeing what she had for sale in the open suitcase that sat on the orange crate in front of her. It didn't help that today's product happened to be stainless-steel apple corers, which weren't exactly at the top of everybody's shopping list. Still, that shouldn't have made any difference. For Evelyn Lolis of the Sandman's Guild, selling had very little to do with the customer wanting to buy.

Well, she couldn't stand here all day. It was time to jump-start the business.

She emitted a short but musical yodel, and a passing businessman turned to investigate the source of the sound. Lolis wasted no time locking eyes with the man and drawing him toward her. When the picture-in-picture image appeared, she knew she had him.

"You need a handy-dandy apple corer," she intoned, holding his gaze. "You need it more than you've ever needed anything in your life. Ten bucks, including tax."

She could have charged any amount, even hundreds. But it was best not to be too greedy. Sooner or later, the buyer would come back to himself. And if he was thoroughly ripped off, he might come back to her — this time with a cop.

The man produced a bill and handed it over. "I'll take one."

Lolis accepted the money. "They make great gifts, too. You should probably buy a couple more. Thank you for your patronage. Now, when your wallet is back in your pocket, you'll forget where you bought these wonderful things and go on with your happy day."

The man walked away, whistling. Another satisfied customer. Thanks to hypnotism, there was no other kind.

Out of habit, she looked around to make sure Axel Braintree wasn't witnessing her transaction. Axel had formed the Sandman's Guild to prevent this kind of commerce from taking place. And he definitely wouldn't have appreciated the way she'd acquired the crate of one hundred apple corers in the first place. She'd bent the truck driver at a stoplight, implanting a post-hypnotic suggestion for him to deliver one of his cartons to this intersection. It had been pure bad luck that she'd wound up with corers instead of iPods. After all, it had said APPLE on the truck. Oh, well — easy come, easy go.

She picked out her next customer. This was going to be easy. She didn't even have to reel him in. He was approaching of his own free will, the brim of his fedora pulled low. He leaned in over the suitcase and removed his hat. Sharp black eyes burned into hers.

She recognized the hawk nose and beetle brows too late to do anything about it. With a gasp, she tried to turn away, but Elias Mako ripped into her mind as surely as if he'd used one of her apple corers. She fought with all her mesmeric power to keep him out, but it was a losing battle. The guild members played at hypnotizing one another, but not one of them was capable of this kind of mental bulldozing. She doubted even Axel could withstand it.

"You are very relaxed," he said in a soft, melodious voice.

"I'm not!" she rasped, biting her lip until she tasted blood. Anything to keep from giving herself over to his control.

His eyes grew huge, boring into her soul. "You are reclining on soft white sand on a beautiful beach. The ocean breeze is fragrant with oleander."

She resisted. "It's New York and it smells like pastrami and garbage!" Then the tropical scent reached her, and she sighed with the sheer joy of it all. Her fear disappeared along with the pain of her mouth. The busy intersection faded away.

"You are Evelyn Lolis of the Sandman's Guild."

"Sand*person*'s Guild." Even totally bent, she stuck up for her belief that there were just as many sandwomen as there were sandmen, and the name of the guild should be changed.

"My mistake," Mako agreed genially. "And now you will tell me what I need to know. Where is Jackson Opus?"

"He left town with his family. Axel is living with them." In her mind, she was not betraying anything.

Elias Mako wasn't the enemy. That was all a misunderstanding, long in the past. They were mind-benders together, one big happy family. And wasn't this sea breeze *wonderful* . . . ?

"Yes, but where did they go? Where are they now?"

"Nobody knows," Lolis replied honestly. "Axel set it up so none of us could spill the beans." She frowned. "Why would he do that? Who'd ever hurt the Opuses?"

"Think," the director of Sentia prodded. "You must have some memory. What is their new name? What part of the country are they hiding in?"

Lolis looked mystified. Mako felt a surge of anger. She wasn't holding out on him. He had gained her trust so completely that she was incapable of comprehending the fact that he meant them harm. And, by God, he did! Jackson Opus could not be allowed to continue to develop his limitless potential.

The interview was over. Still, the Lolis woman represented a connection to Braintree, and therefore to Jax.

"And now," Mako said with a sigh, "I invite you to join the laundry."

She looked puzzled for a moment, which was typical of someone who'd received a hypnotic instruction that could not be carried out. A few seconds later, a dry cleaner's van pulled up. The rear double doors opened and Mako gallantly handed her up to Wilson DeVries, who was waiting among the bundles of clothing to receive her.

The doors slammed shut, and all that remained of Evelyn Lolis was the suitcase of apple corers atop an orange crate on West Thirty-Fourth Street.

The viscous liquid bubbling in the flask over the Bunsen burner looked muddy green, but Jax scribbled *yellow* in his lab notebook. Everything looked muddy when seen through his dark glasses. Even the sunny day outside seemed like a November fog.

He lifted the frames just a little for a peek, and changed *yellow* to *amber* — although it was hard to care about his science grade . . . or any other grade, for that matter. He was beginning to feel like the people in the Arctic Circle who spent six months in darkness every year. It brought on depression. Jax could sympathize with that. He wasn't too thrilled with this new school, new town, and new life. And he was even less thrilled with the reason he was forced to live it.

"Hey, Agnes!" A beefy hand swept the glasses off his nose. They skittered across the counter into a rack of test tubes. "Why don't you lose the shades? You might see something."

"That's *Magnus*," Jax growled, raking the offender with an angry look as he reached for the glasses. He used to be Dopus; now it was Agnes. The one thing that was consistent was he always managed to pick enemies who made fun of his name.

Keith Federov was taller than Jax, with long arms that enabled him to reach over Jax and snatch up the frames before Jax could get to them. "No way, movie star."

When the PIP opened up before Jax, he didn't hesitate. Maybe Axel had created the Sandman's Guild to teach hypnotists to resist using their powers, but there were some things a guy shouldn't have to put up with. Keith had the advantage of size and height. Why shouldn't Jax retaliate with his own special skill?

"You will give me back my glasses," he commanded in a low voice.

"Not unless I get passes to your next red-carpet Hollywood premiere," the big boy sneered at him.

Jax blinked in surprise. How had Keith resisted his instruction? You didn't get defiance from a guy who was bent. Yet there was the PIP of Keith looking back at him.

Or was it? Analyzing the vision before him, Jax concluded that the angle was ever-so-slightly off. And — wasn't that the back of Keith's head in the corner of the view? Which meant . . .

He looked behind Keith to see another kid — a short, squat boy, David somebody — staring into Jax's luminous eyes, totally entranced.

Keith held the glasses over the bubbling beaker. "I wonder if there's any acid in this stuff?"

Oh, well; Axel wasn't going to like this. Jax focused on David and whispered his instructions.

"What are you mumbling about, Agnes?" Keith demanded belligerently.

Behind him, David picked up Keith's notebook and thrust it into the flame of the Bunsen burner.

"Fire!" Jax barked.

Keith wheeled to find his experiment notes ablaze on the countertop. In the chaos that followed, he dropped the sunglasses, and Jax was able to retrieve them and get them back on his nose — but not before murmuring to David, "This wasn't your fault. It was Keith fooling around."

The teacher bounded onto the scene, and the blackened notebook was shrouded in a cloud of fire-extinguisher foam.

"Who did that?" she asked angrily.

Both Jax and David pointed at Keith.

"I never touched that book!" the big boy defended himself. "I was holding . . ." His voice trailed off. He couldn't protest his innocence without admitting that he'd started the fracas in the first place.

Keith was banished to the office. It wasn't justice, Jax reflected, but it was deeply satisfying.

David seemed utterly bewildered, so Jax murmured, "When the bell rings, this whole class was just a blur to you." One of the things he'd learned at Sentia was that it was a good idea to take care of the loose ends.

"You really did a number on Federov."

Jax turned in the passing parade of students. Felicity Green was matching his pace in the crowded hallway. The Greens lived in the house directly behind the Magnuses, separated by two postage-stamp-size backyards.

"What do you mean?" The last thing Jax needed was to attract the attention of this nosy neighbor — especially since they were in three of the same classes.

"Keith's an idiot, but not a lot of people have the guts to stand up to him," she said admiringly. "How did you get your hands on his book without him noticing?"

Jax shrugged. "It all happened really fast."

She grinned appreciatively, which hollowed out a dimple in her left cheek. She was petite and blonde, with a healthy, natural look except for a thin purple streak dyed into her hair. "Did you get your banana bread yet?"

"Banana bread?"

"My mom bakes her famous banana bread for everybody new to the neighborhood," she explained. "She's been working overtime lately, so I wasn't sure if she'd made it to your house. You live with your parents and your grandfather, right?"

Jax edged closer to alert mode. He'd already noticed Felicity spent a lot of time looking out the back window of her house. Now he understood why: She was a natural snoop, curious about everybody's business. That would have been fine. In fact, she seemed genuinely nice. Except that the Magnus family's business didn't bear inspection.

"It's my uncle," Jax told her, sticking to the cover story they'd invented to explain Braintree's presence in their home. "My mom's older brother. He's staying with us for a while."

"He's in really great shape for his age," she commented. "He spends half the day exercising."

"He's into fitness," Jax agreed lamely. "He and my mom are super close."

"Really?" She was surprised. "She says he's driving her crazy."

He stopped in his tracks and turned sharply. "How would you know that?"

“Don’t hate me,” the girl said sheepishly. “I read lips.”

She was hard to hate, but that wasn’t the point. Jax and his family were hiding out here in Haywood. And sheer random chance had landed them across a sixty-foot expanse of grass from the local one-girl CIA.

Sure, Felicity Green meant them no harm. But when Dr. Elias Mako was looking for you, an innocent invasion of privacy could turn into a genuine invasion.

3000 BCE: Large-eyed hieroglyphs on Egyptian obelisk indicate hypnotism.

75 CE: Roman gladiators experiment with mind techniques to improve chances of survival in the arena.

850 CE: Aztec priests mesmerize victims as preparation for human sacrifice.

1066 CE: William the Conqueror changes his name from William, Manipulator of Minds, in order to downplay the role of hypnotism in the conquest of England.

1492 CE: Queen Isabella's post-hypnotic suggestion makes Columbus take a wrong turn, heading west instead of east.

1689 CE: Baron Bartholemeus Sparks throws vast parties featuring large-scale hypnotism of guests by his Sparks relatives. Attendees' memories are erased nightly.

1764 CE: Sir Roland Opus is convicted of treason for mesmerizing a knighthood from King George, hypnotizes the hangman to escape execution, and emigrates to the American colonies by bending a ship's captain.

Jax looked up from the notes he was working on. "We have to stop, Axel. I need to study. I've got a *real* history test on the Minutemen tomorrow, and there's not going to be any hypnotism on it."

Braintree raised a bristly brow. "Is that so? 'One if by land, and two if by sea'? That's a post-hypnotic suggestion if I've ever heard one."

"No kidding!" Jax was impressed. He was only beginning to learn of the many world events that had been shaped by mind-benders over the centuries. And some of the greatest practitioners of the art had been relatives, both on the Opus side and the Sparks — Mom's family. He sighed. "Forget it. If I put that, I'll flunk for sure."

The old man nodded. "John Adams was the most gifted hypnotist ever to hold the office of president. Wait till you hear what he made Jefferson do at the Second Continental Congress."

Jax held his ears. "If I can't tell the difference between the textbook and hypnotic history, we're both going to have some explaining to do on report-card day."

Braintree was firm. "A bad grade is a small price to pay for keeping yourself and your family alive."

"Tell that to my mother."

"She already knows, and so does your father. Your parents gave up their careers to come here, but it was a move they made happily, for your sake. I don't think a bad report card will throw them. Your mother and I may not see eye to eye on much, but we both agree that nothing is more important than keeping you safe from Mako."

Jax squirmed uncomfortably in his desk chair. Not a day went by when he didn't regret how his so-called gift had brought all this down on his family. "How does learning about people who died hundreds of years ago keep me safe from Mako?"

"Studying what has gone before is the only way to prepare yourself for what is yet to come."

"Yeah, but a five-thousand-year-old obelisk?" Jax challenged.

"We were able to prevent your parents from jumping in front of a subway train," the old man explained seriously, "because we understood Mako's utilization of a trigger word for a post-hypnotic suggestion. Sandmen have employed many trigger words over the centuries, like Abraham Lincoln's use of *fourscore*. If I hadn't studied, your mother and father might well have died that day."

Jax knew all too well how close he had come to tragedy in New York. "All right, I get it. I have to learn hypnotic history. But while you're teaching, you might want to stay away from the window. You know that girl, Felicity, who lives across the way? She reads lips."

"I'm sure a pretty young thing like her has better things to do than mind our business."

Jax shook his head. "Apparently not. She knows your exercise routine and exactly what Mom thinks of it. And she sort of senses that we're all uptight about something. It's not good."

Braintree nodded gravely. "If she picks up something about hypnotism, she'll probably assume she's mistaken.

But just to be on the safe side, stay friendly with her. If she comes to any dangerous conclusions, we may have to convince her otherwise."

Jax made a face. "I thought the Sandman's Guild had a rule about that."

"We're not asking for her father's credit-card number. We're just protecting ourselves. And remember to keep your dark glasses on at school."

"I will," Jax promised. "But we've started this new chess program, and they won't let me wear shades. Mr. Isaacs says it's an unfair advantage if your opponent can't see your eyes scanning the board."

"Quit," the old man decided without hesitation. "The chance of unintentional hypnotism is too great."

"No can do. Chess is mandatory for everybody. It's supposed to promote logic and reasoning. And you know what? Turns out I'm pretty good at it. I haven't lost a match yet."

Braintree looked worried. "I'll have to step up your lessons. Sometimes it's harder to avoid a mesmeric connection than to establish one."

"Hey!" Jax was offended. "I'm not bending anybody. I'm winning fair and square."

"Perhaps," the old man agreed without much conviction. "You've always been a smart kid. A sandman needs a canny understanding of the world around him." He seemed lost in thought for a moment, frowning. "What does your mother have against my exercise routine? A healthy body is important to maintaining a powerful mind."

Jax laughed, but stopped abruptly when he glanced out the window and spied a face in the upstairs window of the house across the way. Felicity.

He kept his lips shut.

At the FBI's Cyber Crimes division in Washington, DC, Special Agent Gil Frobisher was staring at carpet samples when his assistant appeared in the doorway.

"Got a minute, Gil?"

Frobisher motioned her inside, but his concentration remained on the samples. "It's supposed to be moss, loden, and asparagus. All I see is green, green, and green."

"The loden is more of an olive shade," Agent Wendy Lee said helpfully.

"Olive — that's another one!" Frobisher began rummaging through the box on the floor next to his desk. In truth, he'd had very little interest in this home renovation until his wife had told him what it was going to cost. For that kind of money, he was interested — even if he couldn't tell smoky topaz from burnt sienna.

Lee cleared her throat. "There's been a development."

Her boss didn't look up from the carton. "The cyberattack in the Balkans?"

"No, the Vote Whisperer."

That got Frobisher's attention. Of all the cases on his plate, he was certain that the Vote Whisperer was destined for the bureau's File 27 — the collection of bizarre and ridiculous complaints that found their way into the folder that came after the *Zs*. The reports had been trickling in since just before the New York primary election — people complaining about a boy's voice coming from computers, tablets, and phones, commanding them to vote for candidate Trey Douglas. The peculiar part was that no one could recall any video accompanying this audio. Stranger still, the Internet users themselves vehemently denied that any such message had been broadcast. The "witnesses" had all been within earshot, but not in sight of the screen.

It was probably nothing, but even if there turned out to be some substance to it, there was no crime involved. Campaign ads were 100 percent legal.

He sighed. "What's up? Another *ear*witness?"

Lee nodded. "But this one heard something none of the others did. Apparently, before the order to vote for Douglas, the voice said, 'You will remember nothing of me or this message.' "

"The plot thickens," Frobisher said without much enthusiasm.

"You know, when I quit smoking," his assistant mused, "I saw a psychologist who specialized in hypnosis. Before he put me under, he walked me through the process. Part of it was commanding the subject to remember nothing."

Her boss sat forward in his chair. "So what are you saying? You think some kid tried to rig an election by hypnotizing people over the Internet? Is that even possible?"

"I just got off the phone with the head of psychiatry at Johns Hopkins. He says no."

"Well, there you go." Frobisher was relieved. "I think we can safely file the Vote Whisperer under 27 along with the Yeti sightings and the tomato that looks like Elvis Presley. Good riddance, too. I've got carpets to pick."

Agent Lee frowned. "But how do you explain so many people reporting the same thing?"

"Because people report things. Like UFOs. And Elvis. And baby stegosauruses digging up their vegetable gardens. If the Johns Hopkins guy says it's impossible, that's good enough for me."

"I guess. Unless . . ."

"Unless what?"

"Unless we're dealing with something *different*," Lee suggested. "You know, something we've never seen before. That happens every now and then, doesn't it?"

Frobisher glared at the Vote Whisperer folder on his desk. It was thin, and he didn't want it to get any thicker. If he took this to his superiors and it turned out to be a whole lot of nothing, *he* would be going into File 27 right along with it. They would demote him down to paper shredder. And on a paper shredder's salary, he'd never be able to afford asparagus-colored carpets.

On the other hand, if he swept this under the rug and it turned out to be big, that would be even worse. And tampering with a free and fair election was about as big as things could get.

"What happened to Trey Douglas in the New York primary? Did he win?"

"You remember," she told him. "He won huge. And

then he dropped out in the middle of his own victory party. Nobody knows why. Even he can't really explain it — just that he's sticking with his decision."

So the Vote Whisperer's candidate had won big. Did that mean anything? Not according to the expert from Johns Hopkins. Yet if Wendy was right, and these were new and uncharted waters, there were no experts.

Campaign ads were perfectly legal, but what if this went a step beyond that? Two words gnawed at the back of his throat, scary words: *mind control.*

One element had to be the key. How had the mysterious message managed to target listeners in the next room while somehow missing people looking directly at their screens?

His FBI instinct told him that he had to have the answer to that question before he could decide the future of the Vote Whisperer case.

"Keep the file open," he said at last.

Felicity Green was the world's first chess cheerleader.

It started on the school bus home. Jax was in his usual position — wedged in a spot near the rear, his sneakers propped against the seat in front of him, hiding behind his sunglasses and his own knees — when Felicity flopped down beside him.

"Hi, Jack! Congrats on your big win!"

He honestly didn't know what she was talking about. "Big win?"

"You pinned Newsome's queen and checkmated him six moves later," she enthused. "You *owned*!"

"Oh — right."

"You've got Mulaly next, table sixteen in the cafeteria. How are you feeling?"

"Uh, pretty good," Jax replied. "I've got kind of a sniffle, but it's probably just allergies."

"Hey!" she announced loudly to the entire bus. "Jack's playing Mulaly tomorrow. I say he takes him down!"

A confused murmur greeted this bold prediction, and a few strange looks were tossed their way. Jax tried to shrink into the corner of the seat.

"I guess chess isn't as rah-rah as football or basketball," he offered lamely.

"Well, it should be. It takes intelligence, skill, and a killer instinct. Everybody's going to see that when you *wreck* Mulaly."

"What if he wrecks me?" Jax offered.

She snorted. "That guy? He eats jelly sandwiches for lunch. That's not brain food."

She didn't know a rook from third base, and she called the pawns "ponds." Yet she turned out to be right. He *did* wreck Mulaly the next day, and DiStefano after that. Kerry DiStefano was known as one of the best players in the school.

"We're really proud, honey," his mother told him after the second week, when Jax found himself at the top of the standings with a perfect record of 8 and 0. "You never took much of an interest in chess before."

Jax shrugged. "Well, I learned the different moves a long time ago. But this is the first time I've played seriously. I guess I've got kind of a knack."

Braintree had a different theory. "I might have an explanation for this 'knack' of yours," the old man said when he and Jax were alone in the attic room.

Jax looked at him sharply. "Don't tell me I'm bending my opponents, because I'm not. I would know."

"There are different levels of mental connection," Braintree lectured. "I'm not talking about a full mesmeric link with a view of yourself back across the chessboard. This would be more like a series of hypnotic hiccups. Your talents are growing by leaps and bounds every day. It's impossible to measure your power based on the abilities of ordinary sandmen."

"You think I'm telling people to lose?" Jax demanded. "I don't open my mouth during these games. Nobody does. You get to say 'check' or 'checkmate' or 'I have to go to the bathroom.' That's all. Even if I'm bending them by accident, I'm not giving them any instructions."

"It's possible that your eyes alone are enough to break their concentration. Or perhaps your gift is so strong that you somehow communicate your desire to win even without speaking the words."

Jax reddened. "You can't stand to let me be good at something, can you?"

"On the contrary," Braintree countered blandly, "you're *very* good at something. It just doesn't happen to be chess. You are the nexus —"

"I don't want to hear about the Opuses and the Sparkses!" Jax exploded angrily. "They were amazing mind-benders — so what? That doesn't mean a couple of them couldn't have been good at chess, too! That great-great-granduncle who convinced Gustave Eiffel to build a big tower in Paris — how do you know it was hypnotism? Maybe it was a bet over a friendly chess match."

"I see you're upset, so we'll drop the subject for now. But it's not wise to draw attention to yourself. I think it's time for you to lose the occasional game."

Jax was appalled. "You're asking me to *throw* a match? I can't do that. We get graded on chess. And besides — it wouldn't look right. I have fans. One fan, anyway."

"Ah, yes. The Green girl. All the more reason to make it happen."

It was impossible to argue with that. On Monday, when Jax went into battle against Tess Hargrove, he was determined to go down in flames. He left his king unprotected, squandered half his pawns, and put his pieces in danger again and again. Tess didn't notice any of it. There was no PIP image — no mesmeric connection. But the girl was working the board like this was Chutes and Ladders.

"You're a beast," Felicity told him, eyes shining with admiration.

Mr. Isaacs had a slightly different take on the situation. "I can't argue with your record, but I'd be lying if I said you were playing great. It's almost as if you're lucky enough to draw every opponent on an off day."

"You said there's no luck in chess," Jax protested.

The teacher looked uncomfortable. "Well, maybe you've got me rethinking my position on that."

Jax was forced to face the fact that Braintree was right. He wasn't bending his opponents in the usual sense. Yet, somehow, he was exerting a kind of mesmeric influence over them. It proved that he was no chess master, but it also meant something more sinister: There was nothing he could do, no game he could play, no activity he could turn his hand to, that wouldn't be tainted by this so-called gift.

If I took up stamp collecting, I'd hypnotize the glue off the stamps.

His one consolation was that the chess program was coming to an end, building up to an inevitable showdown between Jax and perennial champion Seth Vanderboom. Felicity assured Jax that the kids of Haywood had been watching Seth annihilate the competition since first grade.

"I can't wait to see you mop the floor with him," she said with relish.

Jax sighed. He had long since given up trying to tone down her enthusiasm. She was determined to cheer him all the way to the pinnacle of middle-school chess-dom. And after leaving his entire life behind him in New York, he had to admit that it was nice to have a pretty girl think he was special — even if she thought it for the wrong reason.

"Listen, Felicity, I really appreciate your — uh — support. But I don't want to make a big deal out of this game with Seth."

"I got you," she said conspiratorially. "You don't want to psych yourself out, thinking the championship of the whole school is on the line."

For Jax, who had recently faced nothing less than his own death and the deaths of his parents at the hands of Dr. Mako, the coming match hardly qualified as high stakes. But he could never explain that to Felicity, so he just agreed with her. He was starting to see that life was a whole lot easier when you did.

In Spanish class, he was shocked when a girl he didn't even know clucked disapprovingly at him. "Yeah, you're working hard now, but you're not going to be prepared for the big game with Seth."

Jax stared at her. "How could you know that?"

"Felicity said you watched TV for three solid hours last night!"

"Yeah, man," added Randy Cruz. "You're not going to take down Seth like that."

Jax could feel his precious low profile rising. He couldn't seem to lose at chess, and he couldn't seem to prevent Felicity from making a big deal out of his winning. He was destined to be famous against his will. The only way to avoid the championship would be to quit. And at this point, walking away would create more of a brouhaha than victory. His sole hope was that Seth, who was a shy loner, would keep his attention on the board and escape the hypnotic effect of Jax's eyes.

As soon as Jax sat down opposite Seth, he knew it was already over.

The boy appeared glazed and preoccupied, and his opening moves seemed random, if not outright dumb. Jax actually toyed with the idea of bending him for real and commanding him to concentrate and play like the champion he was. But he couldn't figure out a way to deliver these instructions with so many people watching. Thanks to his press agent, Felicity, half the school was there, packed onto basketball bleachers, watching and listening. This thing was turning into the Silent Super Bowl. He tried a few pointless moves and a couple of outright blunders, but Seth wasn't taking the bait. With a sigh, he realized that the merciful thing to do was just to win it quickly and take it like a man. At least then chess "season" would be over and the students of Haywood Middle School could find something else to be obsessed with.

It turned out to be not quite so simple. At the word "checkmate," Felicity leaped from the first row of bleachers, threw her arms around Jax, and screamed, "Victory parade!" It wasn't exactly that, but enough kids stormed the court to create a decent amount of chaos. Jax barely got his sunglasses on before the yearbook photographer started snapping pictures.

Axel's not going to be happy about this, Jax thought. *But at least it'll all blow over in a day or two.*

"Congratulations on a well-played game," Mr. Isaacs said without much conviction. "I thought you were done for when you left your queen open to that knight fork. But I guess Seth didn't see it."

"I was surprised by that, too," Jax agreed, deadpan. "I'm just happy it's all over and I can hang up my — uh — pawns."

"What are you talking about, Magnus?" the teacher queried, frowning. "Our champion goes on to the tri-county tournament. I was assuming it would be Seth, but now it's you."

Jax experienced a brief dizzy spell. "I don't have to, right? I can drop out and Seth can take my place."

"This isn't the Miss America pageant. The runner-up doesn't perform your duties if you can't make it."

"But he's *better* than me," Jax pleaded.

"Then he would have beaten you," the teacher said curtly.

Jax's face twisted. "I just think he'd do better against those other kids than he played against me." It sounded lame and he knew it.

"It's you or nobody, Magnus. The tournament's next weekend. I suggest you do some studying — especially your endgames. Please take this seriously. You'll be facing some of the stiffest competition in the state."

Axel Braintree was a convicted art thief who had mesmerized the parole board into granting him early release. Once out of prison, he'd founded the Sandman's Guild to help fellow hypnotists resist the temptation to use their powers for personal gain and nefarious purposes. In no time at all, monthly meetings had filled the back room of the E-Z Wash Laundromat in Manhattan. Sandmen had lined up to confess to mesmeric con games, petty crimes, fraud, pickpocketing, and bending undeserved tips and bonuses from innocent victims. It had turned out to be easy to convince the members to confess their sins; getting them to change their ways was still a work in progress. It was one day at a time, Braintree realized. And now that he was no longer in New York to run the meetings personally, he feared that his sandmen might fall off the wagon for good.

While in hiding with the Opuses, his only contact with the guild was from the one pay telephone in Haywood — outside the 7-Eleven on Main Street. It had been raining all day, and he hunkered under a plastic grocery bag that did not quite cover his dripping ponytail. He had a cell phone, but cell phones were traceable. If Elias

Mako found him, it would be as good as a GPS navigation system straight to Jax. And that could not be allowed to happen.

Only one mind-bender alive had the power to stand up to Mako. Jax was young and raw, but his combination of Opus and Sparks DNA had already given him the ability to do something that was once considered impossible: Jax could hypnotize remotely, via a TV or computer screen. One day, he would overpower Mako — but not if Sentia's director had the opportunity to crush him first.

"How was the meeting last night?" Braintree was asking. "Did you get a nice turnout?"

"Standing room only." Ivan Marcinko was also on a pay phone. In New York City they were much easier to find. "Gresalfi Brothers sent over free pizza. Of course, they thought they were feeding the Salvation Army."

"How could you use hypnotism to get food for a guild meeting, of all things?" the old man scolded.

"I didn't," Marcinko defended himself. "I just *lied*."

Braintree held his head. "Well, it's nice to know you had good attendance, even with me out of the picture." In the interest of security, he never mentioned Haywood or even Connecticut.

"How's the dry cleaning?" More code-speak. Jax was the dry cleaning. His parents were the groceries. Together, the family unit was "my errands."

"Safe, for now. I'm concerned about a few — stains." Jax's newfound chess career was very much on Braintree's mind, but there was no code word for that. Braintree had worked out a few strategies to ensure that Jax made a poor showing at the tri-county tournament, which would be wrapping up any minute. "And the groceries don't always agree with me. Let's just say there may be . . . food allergies involved."

Marcinko cleared his throat on the other end of the line. "Evelyn Lolis wasn't at the meeting last night. I asked around. Nobody's seen her for a long time."

"Well, that's not unusual. Evelyn marches to the beat of a different metronome —"

"She missed a business appointment yesterday," Marcinko interrupted.

A hint of suspicion crept into the old man's voice. "And you know this because . . ."

"I'm her partner."

"She's a waitress; you're a TV salesman. How could you possibly be business partners?"

"Since we both happen to be between jobs at the moment —"

"You mean you got fired," Braintree amended.

"We're producing a Broadway play."

"A Broadway play?"

"It's just in the early stages," Marcinko admitted. "You know, lining up investors. We had a meeting with the wife of a very prominent Wall Street banker, and Evelyn didn't show up."

Light dawned on the president of the Sandman's Guild. "You're *bending* people into investing in a play that doesn't exist so you can take their money!"

"It exists," Marcinko said stubbornly. "It just doesn't exist *yet*."

"Don't con a con man, Ivan. I've been in jail."

"You're missing the point. This whole thing was Evelyn's idea. She set up the investors' meeting. I'm worried about her."

"Maybe her conscience was bothering her. Maybe she remembered what the guild is supposed to be about." Braintree looked at his watch. "I have to go pick up the dry cleaning. Keep your ears open for her. I'll try to call at the same time tomorrow." He hung up and got into his 1999 Dodge Avenger.

The old man had been in New York City more than three decades, and hadn't held a valid license since his stint in prison. The Avenger had been the cheapest vehicle on Ashton Opus's used-car lot.

He began to lurch around the streets, accelerating unsteadily and slamming on the brakes too hard. After thirty years, he was none too skilled behind the wheel.

The chess tournament was at Bolton High School, which was less than ten minutes away. He left the Avenger in an empty part of the lot. It was a long walk to the school, but he hadn't quite mastered parking yet. All those cars so close together — how did people manage it?

As he trudged into the building, he made an effort to control his irritation. It was easy to forget that Jax was only twelve. Naturally, the kid wanted to feel success at something, despite the truth that it had little to do with his skill as a chess player. He would learn soon enough that hypnotism played at least some part in all aspects of his life. Every A he received from a teacher, every girl who agreed to be his prom date, even the love and support of his own parents — none of it could be trusted 100 percent.

The good news, Braintree reflected, following signs to the cafeteria, was that nobody cared about a middle-school chess tournament. So it was no harm done.

He turned the corner into the lunchroom and stopped dead. There stood Jax, triumphantly brandishing a trophy that was at least three feet tall. A reporter held a microphone under his nose as a TV videographer recorded the interview.

". . . well, I was a little nervous when he used the Sicilian Defense," Jax was saying, "but I was able to fight back."

Without hesitation, Braintree inserted himself between Jax and the camera.

"Hey, Grandpa!" the reporter barked angrily. "We're in the middle of an interview here."

The founder of the Sandman's Guild fixed his experienced gaze on the videographer, hypnotizing him quickly. "The object you hold just burst into flames," he intoned in a low voice.

With a yelp, the man let go of the camera. It shattered at his feet, sending pieces in all directions.

"What are you doing, Bernie?" The reporter dropped to his knees and began scuttling after rolling components. "That's an expensive piece of equipment!"

Bernie rubbed his hands together vigorously. "I need ice!"

"Ice?"

In the confusion, Braintree hustled the chess champion and his trophy out of the cafeteria.

"You just broke your own rules," Jax accused.

"He had video of you — talking about where you live and what school you go to."

Jax was sulky. "I doubt Dr. Mako watches Haywood TV."

"And if the station posts the clip on their website? Your biggest fan, Felicity, will have it on YouTube in a heartbeat. You think Mako doesn't have his young disciples searching all media for you?"

"Can I keep the trophy?" Jax asked in a sheepish voice.

Axel Braintree heaved a sigh. "You can put it in a dark corner, away from the nearest window," he said finally. "It's a very nice trophy. Congratulations."

There was at least one thing to celebrate: Jack Magnus's chess career was over.

"Great news, Magnus," Mr. Isaacs said in homeroom the following Wednesday. "You've been selected to play in the Connecticut Invitational All-Star Tournament!"

Jax couldn't suppress the delighted grin that took over his face. "Really? Is that good?"

"Well, I've never heard of this one," the teacher admitted. "But that's probably because nobody from Haywood has ever qualified before. It's on Saturday, up by Avon. You can make it, right?"

"I'll have to check with my family."

"Tell them not to worry about transportation. I'll pick you up around eight, and get you home safe and sound." Mr. Isaacs beamed. "You know, at first I thought you were a mediocre player — that you just happened to draw weak opponents, and catch the strong ones on an off day. But there's a simplicity to your game that's almost brilliant. You lull the competition into a false sense of security until they do something stupid. You're going to put Haywood chess on the map."

"I absolutely forbid it," Braintree said later that night. "We barely kept you off the TV last weekend, and we couldn't stop the *Haywood Gazette* from printing an article. That has to be where this new tournament got your name."

"You know, this time I think I agree with Axel," Mrs. Opus chimed in. "Newspapers, TV — that negates the whole purpose of why we came here."

"I won't do any interviews," Jax promised. "I probably won't even win."

"On the other hand," Mr. Opus countered, "Jax seems to be showing a real knack for this. Why should we stifle his talent?"

"I explained that to you," Braintree said patiently. "He's not playing chess; he's playing the other players. If you examine your own family history, you'll find dozens of virtuosos who did exactly the same thing."

"I don't remember hearing about any chess masters." Ashton Opus didn't like to discuss his heritage. It had not been pleasant to grow up as the non-hypnotic child of two talented mind-benders. "There were some good poker players, though. Maybe too good. I think one of them got shot in a saloon in the Old West."

The old man pleaded with them. "You people gave up everything so you could come here and hide. Why would you let Jax wave himself around in the public eye?"

Jax's mind was made up. "I already said yes to Mr. Isaacs. If anybody tries to interview me, I'll bend him to pick somebody else. It'll be *fine*."

"I'm trying to remember where I've heard those words before." The old man sighed. "Oh, yes — that's what they said aboard the *Hindenburg*."

The GPS in Mr. Isaacs's Hyundai drew them farther north into Connecticut, past Hartford into a wooded area of large stately homes nestled among mature trees. It seemed a lot wealthier here than in Haywood, although a city kid like Jax didn't have much of a basis of comparison. There were plenty of rich people in Manhattan, but these classic New England towns had a different vibe — older and more dignified, the kind of places where movies were set.

"So this is how the other half lives," Mr. Isaacs commented, seeing Jax peering out the window.

"I guess." The teacher could not have known that Ashton Opus's clients at the Bentley dealership had been the other half of the other half — rappers and Wall Street big shots, West Asian princes and movie stars. Jax had never worshipped his father's famous customers, but it made him sad to think about how far the family had fallen, thanks to him.

Past the main drag of Avon, they seemed to leave civilization altogether, entering what appeared to be a vast forest preserve.

At that moment, the GPS announced, *"Arriving at destination."*

Jax was taken aback. "Where — here?"

Mr. Isaacs craned his neck. "Who holds a chess tournament in the Hundred Acre Wood?"

The forest suddenly parted to reveal two towering wrought-iron gates designed with an elaborate pattern of leaves around a large letter *Q*. With a buzz and a crack, the *Q* separated in the middle as the impressive portal began to swing open.

"Whoa," Jax breathed.

The teacher maneuvered in through the gates onto a vast estate that was more on the scale of a national park. Although outside the twenty-five-foot fence was dense forest, the property itself was all rolling lawns, manicured with golf-course care. The Hyundai wound along a meandering road past large topiary animals. A ten-foot-high bear seemed to be reaching for Jax through the passenger window as they passed by.

"There must be a building here somewhere," Mr. Isaacs mused, brow furrowed.

As if on cue, they crested a rise and there it was. The word *mansion* didn't do it justice; it was more like a palace. Not the kind with towers and turrets, but a gigantic stone home that reminded Jax of the Museum of Natural History, or perhaps the White House on steroids.

It was easily half a mile to the point where the drive wrapped around the front fountains, which would have more than filled a football field.

The teacher frowned. "Where is everybody?"

There was only one other car on the drive. Jax recognized it from his father's ex-dealership in Manhattan: a high-end Bentley limousine. With a price tag around six hundred thousand dollars, it probably wasn't the carpool vehicle that had brought some of the other chess players. It belonged to the owner of this house, whoever that might be.

"Maybe there's a parking lot out back," Jax suggested. "You know, for the normal cars."

The cast-bronze front doors of the house swung wide, and out stepped a broad-shouldered man in his thirties, dressed in an impeccably tailored black suit.

As he approached the Hyundai, Mr. Isaacs lowered the passenger window, leaned over the seat, and called, "We're here for the chess tournament. This is the place, right?"

It was a valid question, but it seemed like pulling up to Buckingham Palace and asking the Grenadier Guards where the chili cook-off was.

"You must be Mr. Isaacs. And Jack Magnus. You can leave the car and I'll show you inside."

Teacher and student shared a look. What kind of tournament was so well run that they recognized not only the contestants but their drivers as well?

At the front door, Jax wiped his feet about twenty times. If he tracked mud into this place, it might unlock a hidden reservoir of Mom-guilt that would overwhelm him.

The house was cavernous, with endless anterooms, and staircases spiraling off into what looked like ceilingless space. Jax was pretty sure he recognized some of the paintings from art class. He might have been wrong, but his teacher was gazing around the place absolutely pop-eyed.

"That's a Vermeer," he mumbled to Jax. "A real one!"

"My employer is an avid collector," the man informed them. "Perhaps there will be time for you to tour the galleries."

"Where's the tournament going to be held?" Mr. Isaacs asked.

"And where are all the other players?" Jax added.

"My employer invites you to join him for breakfast" was the only reply.

The teacher stopped in his tracks. "Is there a chess tournament here today?"

"I prefer to allow my employer to provide that explanation."

Mr. Isaacs dug in his heels. "I'm responsible for my student. His parents gave him to me so he could play chess. If that's not going to happen, we have to leave."

"Well, then we'll have to tie you to your chairs and force-feed you oatmeal!" came a papery voice in an amused tone. "Cut the cloak-and-dagger, Zachary."

Zachary stepped aside to reveal the speaker — an ancient man in a high-tech wheelchair, frail and a little shaky, yet absolutely confident in the way of the very wealthy. Tubes and wires were attached to his body, and he was flanked by two nurses who monitored gauges and readouts all around him. His skin matched an elephant's in both color and wrinkle content, yet there was something alight in his face — intelligence, even youth.

"You'll have to excuse Zachary," their host apologized. "He's the perfect gentleman's gentleman. Problem is *I'm* no gentleman. Avery Quackenbush. Forgive me for not getting up. I might blow a gasket on all this fancy machinery."

Mr. Isaacs goggled. "Avery Quackenbush the media tycoon?"

"No, Avery Quackenbush the sewer cleaner." When he grinned, it stretched the skin tight over the bones of his face, giving him a skeletal appearance. "I got all this stuff clipping money-saving coupons."

A high-pitched giggle escaped Jax. Whatever this old buzzard wanted, he was a pretty funny guy.

"I don't mean to be disrespectful," the teacher put in quickly. "But I'm supposed to be taking Jack to a chess tournament. This obviously isn't it. What exactly are we doing here?"

The billionaire waved it off. "No need to apologize. People have been disrespectful to me for ninety-six years. It rolls right off me like water off a duck's back. There's no tournament here today, but I had Zachary pick up a really nice trophy in case you have to prove that you've been to one. I'm an old man, and the enjoyments left to me in this life you could count on the fingers of one hand. Is it too much to ask to play a game against this young chess master I've been reading about in the papers?"

Jax spoke up. "Why me? No offense, but you could afford to fly in the world chess champion or buy yourself that IBM supercomputer that beat him."

The old man's laugh was like someone crushing cellophane. "I'm a terrible chess player. I couldn't hold a candle to the champ or Deep Blue. But I might be able to beat a kid."

Jax regarded his teacher. "Would it be okay?"

Mr. Isaacs sighed. "Well, it's not what we came here for. But if you want to give Mr. Quackenbush a game, I can't see any harm in it."

Zachary cleared his throat. "A light breakfast is served in the solarium."

The "light" breakfast turned out to be an elaborate buffet prepared by the billionaire's personal chef. Jax wasn't hungry, and Quackenbush's ill health prevented him from enjoying a hearty meal. Leaving the teacher attending to a heaping plate of eggs Florentine, the two chess players repaired to an adjoining games room. They sat down across an elegant set carved in ivory and onyx.

The pieces were smooth, perfectly weighted, and a pleasure to handle. Jax had the billionaire over a barrel in slightly less than eleven minutes. Avery Quackenbush had told the truth — he was a terrible player.

The billionaire took it all in good spirits and laid down his king a few moves before checkmate. "Well, you killed me." He indicated the tubes and apparatus all around him. "Of course, I'm nine-tenths dead anyway."

Jax flushed. What could he possibly say to something like that? "You look fabulous"? It would be an obvious lie. "I'm sorry" was all he could manage.

"What are you sorry about?" Quackenbush cackled. "I'm the one who's dying." The laughter morphed into a racking cough. The nurses stepped forward, but he waved them off — all the way out of the room. "We need a little privacy before your keeper polishes off his eggs. No, no — don't set up the pieces again. We have something to talk about." He reached into a pocket on the side of his wheelchair, produced a photograph, and laid it on the chessboard.

Jax examined the picture. His own face stared directly back at him, his eyes intense and deep purple. Why was the billionaire showing him a picture of himself? And where had he gotten it? Jax had never even heard of Avery Quackenbush before today. He tried in vain to recall when such a picture might have been taken, but there was no frame of reference. His face filled most of the image; the background was sterile and white —

Oh, no . . .

Recognition staggered him and blurred his vision for a moment. This was no posed photograph. It was a computer screenshot of the video Dr. Mako had forced Jax to record.

What floored Jax was that this picture existed at all. Mako had created a security mechanism within the video virus. Once the message was delivered, the hypnotized recipient was instructed to forget it immediately. The viewer would be bent, and therefore powerless to disobey. Then the computer pop-up would disappear, and the message would self-erase. According to Mako's planning, this screenshot should not exist. Whoever took it should have been unaware that there was anything to take a picture of.

"Where did you get this?" Jax asked in a small voice.

The billionaire shrugged. "I could spend my money on rock-climbing gear, but I don't think I'd get much use out of it. But private eyes, eggheads, hackers, snitches — they can find anything. As you can see, I don't have much quality of life hooked up to tubes and wires and gauges; I don't have much health, and I know I don't have much time. What I do have is resources. This picture isn't as important as what it says about its subject."

"Which is?"

"I'm not looking for Jack Magnus, the chess champ. I need Jackson Opus, the hypnotist."

Jax fought down a wild impulse to run. How would he ever explain it to Mr. Isaacs, who was probably still stuffing his face? And even if he could convince the teacher to make a break for it, he could never hide from this eccentric billionaire and his private eyes, eggheads, hackers, and snitches. The suffocating feeling of being trapped kept him pinned to his chair.

"I — I don't know what you're talking about."

"The ship's already sailed on that one, Jackson — or should I say Jax?" Mr. Quackenbush told him briskly. "I haven't got time to trade tall tales. That special talent of yours won the election for Trey Douglas. And if he hadn't been stupid enough to drop out of the race, he probably would have been president. But I've got more important things on my plate than which wing nut gets to sit in the Oval Office. I need your help."

He knows, Jax thought to himself. *He knows exactly who I am and what I did.* He couldn't imagine how, but maybe it was true that money really did buy you everything. He pondered his options. Playing dumb wasn't working. The old guy already had too much information.

Jax could bend him and try to erase all memory of Jackson Opus. But what then? He couldn't very well track down all the billionaire's famous private eyes, eggheads, hackers, and snitches and erase *their* memories, too. Sooner or later, Mr. Quackenbush would be back up to speed, this time mad as a hornet at the kid who'd hypnotized him.

No, the only choice was to hear the man out.

"What do you want?" Jax asked finally.

"I'm a train wreck," Quackenbush explained. "You don't have to protest to make me feel better. What's more, I'm a train wreck with a time limit. I've got the best doctors money can buy, and they give me a month, six weeks at the outside."

In spite of his unease, Jax felt genuine sympathy for his host. "What is it?"

The simple act of shrugging seemed to cost the tycoon great effort. "It's everything. The whole shooting match. Heart, lungs, liver, kidneys. CSS, they call it — Catastrophic Systemic Shutdown."

"I'm really sorry," Jax said, and meant it. "Is there any hope at all?"

"I've got a team of researchers working on the problem night and day. And they're getting really close to a promising treatment for my condition."

"That's great!" Jax exclaimed. "Uh — isn't it?"

"It *would* be," Quackenbush agreed. "If I live long enough to receive it. But it's at least four months away. And if I've got six weeks . . . You do the math. Funny thing about money — you can hire all the overpaid, overeducated nerds in the world, but you can't buy five extra minutes if it's not in the cards."

Jax studied the squares of the chessboard. It was the saddest thing he'd ever heard, even coming from a ninety-six-year-old. He would never have imagined himself capable of such sympathy for someone who had already been given nearly a century and all the wealth, success, and power anyone could want. Yet here was Avery Quackenbush — like any other person — seeing the end and clinging to precious life.

Then the tycoon spoke five words Jax had not been expecting: "That's where you come in."

"Me?"

"I'm hiring you to come here every day and hypnotize me."

Jax could not have been more astounded if Quackenbush had asked him to levitate the mansion off its foundations. "You mean to command you to *not die*? It doesn't work that way!"

The billionaire chuckled. "If only it were that easy. No, I need you to put me in a trance so deep that the relaxation will slow down my metabolism. I've talked to experts who believe that you might be able to put my entire body into some kind of power-save mode. Think of the way animals that hibernate downshift their whole life force to a minimum during the winter. Well, if you could manage that, I might be able to stretch out my six weeks into the months I need."

Jax was thunderstruck. "And your doctors say that could work?"

"Some of them. But if even one of them says it's possible, what have I got to lose? Money? I've already got more than I know what to do with. And, anyway, there's nowhere to spend it where I'm going."

"But I'm not a doctor," Jax protested. "I haven't even finished seventh grade. A few months ago, I thought hypnotism was a stage trick! If you're betting your life on me, it's a gamble even you can't afford."

"You let me worry about the odds," Quackenbush told him. "If you can control millions of people over the Internet, you've got a better chance of pulling this off than anybody else."

Jax tried a different approach. "But I have parents. I go to school. How am I going to get here every day? It's too far for me to ride my bike." Even as he spoke, he thought of the Bentley and the multiple garage doors at the side of the mansion. Transportation would hardly be a problem.

"Let's sweeten the pot a little," the billionaire suggested with a sly glance. "If you give me what I need, I'll set up a trust fund to pay your family five hundred thousand dollars a year for life, regardless of what happens to me."

Jax was certain that all the Opus and Sparks DNA in the world couldn't accomplish what Quackenbush had in mind. Yet as soon as he heard the proposal, he knew he was going to accept it. How could he pass up the chance to win security for Mom and Dad, who had given up so much for the sake of their son? To get out of that awful house, out of those depressing jobs — maybe out of the country, far from Elias Mako. He owed it to Braintree, too, who was stuck in the attic when his heart was in the back of a Manhattan laundromat with his sandmen. It would be a win-win for everyone. And if it turned out — as Jax suspected — that he couldn't do anything to prolong the life of the sick old man, it was still worth a try. How could it ever be bad to help somebody, even if your effort might be doomed from the start?

"Well, I have to ask my parents first," he said finally. "And — uh — my uncle."

"You have twenty-four hours," the billionaire informed him in the tone of someone who was used to making the rules.

"What if I need more time?" Jax wheedled, dreading the prospect of explaining all this to Mom and Dad, much less Braintree.

"Time is the one thing I can't afford," Quackenbush said briskly. "We'll start Monday. Zachary will pick you up after school."

Jax gulped. The tycoon didn't take no for an answer.

"I'll have my lawyer start setting up the trust." Quackenbush pressed a button on the wheelchair and the two nurses reappeared immediately, checking dials and readouts. "When my blood pressure gets to two hundred," he quipped, "sell."

The two women laughed politely.

Mr. Isaacs appeared in the doorway. "I thought you two were supposed to be playing chess," he commented a little suspiciously.

Jax did the only thing he could think of. Braintree definitely wouldn't approve, but the business of today had to remain secret, especially to Mr. Isaacs, who knew him as Jack Magnus, middle-school chess champion.

He stood up and fixed his eyes on the teacher. The PIP image appeared almost immediately, vivid and in surprising detail. "You're very tired, Mr. Isaacs. You've had an exciting day watching a really hard-fought chess tournament. I didn't win, but I gave it my all, battling to the end. I came in third place. You're proud of me."

The nurses were engrossed in the various instruments on the chair, and barely seemed to notice. Quackenbush, however, was greatly interested. "That's all there is to it?"

Jax hushed him with a finger to his lips, and the billionaire fell silent, chastened. It was probably the first time in many decades that anyone had dared to admonish this titan of industry.

"We're going to leave now," Jax went on to the teacher. "When we pass through the gates of the estate, you'll wake up refreshed and excited after a really fun competition in a crowded high-school gym. You'll have no recollection of meeting Avery Quackenbush or setting foot inside his home."

"No loose ends," the tycoon approved. "I like your style, kid."

A few minutes later, as the Hyundai merged onto the main road, Mr. Isaacs peered over at Jax. "I hope you're not too disappointed that you lost in the quarterfinals."

"I'm cool with it," Jax replied blandly. "You taught me a lot about being a good sport."

"Avery Quackenbush!" Mr. Opus exclaimed. "I thought he died years ago!"

Although Jax had never heard of the billionaire before today, to the adults in the rental home, the Quackenbush name was a household word, right up there with Bill Gates and the Rockefellers. There were small countries with full UN membership that didn't have as much money as Jax's new employer.

"He probably would have," Jax agreed, "if he didn't have a team of doctors and nurses keeping him alive. Now he thinks his only hope is me."

"You?" his mother blurted. "I can't depend on you to take out the garbage, and one of the richest men in the world thinks you're going to save his life?"

"He just needs to hang on for a few more months — until his private researchers can develop this new treatment they're working on. He thinks I can hypnotize him so deeply that his life force will slow down — like an animal in hibernation." He turned to face the fourth person at the kitchen table. "Is that even possible? I mean, can hypnotism do that?"

Axel Braintree glanced over his shoulder to confirm that the kitchen blinds were shut. This was not the kind of conversation that lip-reading Felicity Green should be able to look in on.

"I've never heard of it," he replied thoughtfully, "but that doesn't mean it can't be done. It would require an extremely powerful mesmeric connection. And you'd have to maintain the link much longer than usual."

"Wait a minute," Mr. Opus interjected. "You're *considering* this?"

"It's half a million bucks, Dad," Jax informed his father. "Every year, forever. I changed our lives to *this*." He indicated the shabby kitchen. "This is my chance to do better — for all of us."

"If anything happens to you, half a million dollars won't make our lives better," his mother retorted nervously. "Neither would half a *trillion*. I've got nothing against money, but don't you see how *weird* this is? How does Avery Quackenbush, of all people, suddenly need our twelve-year-old son? It's bizarre!"

"It's worse than that," Braintree put in grimly. "That same Avery Quackenbush knows what Jax can do. He knows his real name, and he was able to pluck him off a plate like a shrimp dumpling."

"Well, a man like Quackenbush has access to all the private detectives money can buy," Mr. Opus reasoned.

"That's not the point," the old man insisted. "If he found Jax, that means Jax is *findable*. It's probably only a matter of time until others find him, too — others like Mako."

An icy chill descended over the table. They could debate the pros and cons of working for Quackenbush. But there was little doubt about the fate that awaited Jax should he fall into the hands of Sentia's director.

"Does this mean we have to move again?" asked Jax's mother in a small voice.

Braintree considered the question. "Not yet," he answered finally. "But this should be a lesson to all of us. That time might very well come, and we have to be prepared for it. Mako may not have the resources of a billionaire, but his reach is very long."

"All the more reason I have to do this," Jax decided. "When the time comes that we have to disappear again, it'll be a lot easier to do it if we have money."

The Opuses eventually agreed, as Jax had known that they would. It only added to his guilt. Not only had they been robbed of their careers and identities; now they were no longer capable of making decisions for the family. That job had fallen to a son who was not yet even a teenager and Braintree, an oddball, intrusive stranger. Worse, they were non-hypnotic people wrapped up in the intrigues of mind-benders — exposed to the dangers, yet incapable of affecting their own fate. Dad was armed only with his memories of parents he was certain had been hypnotizing him to eat his vegetables and do his homework. Mom had even less than that — her Sparks ancestors had been inactive in mesmerism for generations. All she knew was that she had surrendered her well-ordered life to something she could not see, feel, or understand.

Of course, Jax had the ability to win every argument with his parents before it even started. All he really needed to do was bend them into seeing things his way. But he'd made a conscious decision never to resort to that unless their lives were on the line. Sooner or later, Mom and Dad would figure out he was manipulating them, and they'd never trust him again. The last thing he needed was parents who didn't dare look him in the eye. Life was weird enough already.

Braintree was not finished with his young protégé. "The kind of hypnotic connection you are about to enter into could be extremely dangerous," he told Jax when they were alone in the attic. "A mesmeric link is not meant to be sustained for the time it will probably take to induce the deep state of relaxation Quackenbush is seeking."

Jax nodded. "That happened to me once at Sentia. I got too far into somebody's head."

"That experience will seem like a tiny cough in comparison to what lies ahead. The mind you'll be entering is a museum housing nearly a century of memories and experiences, both exultant and tragic. The range of emotions will be enormous — unimaginable success, bitter conflict, crushing loss. Your twelve years of life cannot possibly prepare you for the onslaught that will be coming at you."

Jax looked worried. "What can I do to protect myself?"

"I'll work with you," Braintree promised. "But right now, I'm due at the pay phone. I'm expecting an update from New York."

Jax watched him leave the house, back out of the driveway, and weave unsteadily down the road. The way the old guy drove, he could only hope that there would still *be* an Axel Braintree when the time came for his prep session.

The investors were getting nervous, and that meant Ivan Marcinko was even more nervous.

It should have been simple: Hypnotize people into believing that a Broadway play was in production — a theater rented, a cast in rehearsal, an opening planned. Foolproof.

Except for one problem: Evelyn was nowhere to be found.

Where was she? She'd missed the last four meetings! And while she could be a little flaky, where money was concerned, she was smooth as glass! If she wasn't holding her end up, something had to be very wrong.

That's what he was planning to tell Braintree as he strode to the pay phone on Seventh Avenue. He'd suspected it before, and now he was positive: Evelyn was in trouble.

Marcinko reached the corner and stopped short. The pay phone was occupied. He checked the time. Braintree would be expecting his call. He approached the man and tapped his watch, indicating that he was waiting. The man gave no sign that he'd noticed — his features were concealed behind aviator glasses and a fedora pulled low. Marcinko grimaced in annoyance. The guy was wearing a magnificently tailored topcoat that probably cost four thousand dollars. If anyone could afford a top-of-the-line cell phone, it was him. Cheapskate! Where did he get off hogging regular people's pay phones?

He leaned into the man's face and said, "Got an emergency here, friend."

The man flipped up the aviator glasses. The eyes that were suddenly trained on Marcinko burned deep inside his brain, clutching for control with stunning force and speed.

Mako!

Marcinko would have been instantly bent if the strength of the onslaught hadn't sent him staggering backward. He crashed into a mailbox, and the pain of the collision doubled him over, breaking the eye contact. Panic-stricken, he turned and ran, knowing he dared not look back for fear that those eyes would seize him again and he would be lost.

He sensed rather than heard Mako's footsteps behind him, but there was no urgency there, no real chase. Why?

A moment later, he had his explanation. A powerful blow struck him from the side, driving him into a blind alley. The attack dropped him to the litter-strewn pavement, and he looked up to see a boy not much older than the Opus kid, but twice Jax's size, built like a football player.

Marcinko raised his fists to fight back, but it soon became clear that the brawl was not going to be a physical one. Wilson DeVries gazed down at him with a mesmeric punch equal to the tackle that had put him in the alley.

Marcinko battled back, sealing his mind to the intrusion. He was a match for this teenager, and perhaps more than a match. Marcinko was not the most naturally talented sandman, but he had one advantage — the experience of using his gift to scratch out a living against all odds — and no kid had that. Slowly, he began to see his own image appear as he bulled his way into the boy's mind.

"Listen to me," he breathed. "The next time you see Elias Mako, knock his teeth down his throat! He's your enemy! Do it to him before he does it to you. . . ."

It almost worked.

Mako turned the corner and stepped into the gloom of the alley just in time to spot Wilson's haymaker coming his way.

Mako said one word: "Stop."

There was no time for Sentia's director to hypnotize Wilson, who was already under Marcinko's power. Yet the dark eyes crackled with such ferocity, his voice resounded with such command, that the meaty fist froze in midair an inch from Mako's jaw.

Then he transferred his electrifying attention to the trapped sandman, who was helpless to do anything more than stare back. "That's better," said a mellow voice, almost kindly. "Be a good boy and come with me."

It sounded enormously reasonable, even inviting. But as Marcinko got up and followed Mako and Wilson to a waiting limousine, a tiny thought still nagged from a distant corner of his brain: that whatever had happened to Evelyn Lolis must have started exactly this way.

10

The Quackenbush Bentley was parked in the main drive of the school on Monday afternoon, blocking the bus lane as if that was the privilege of one of the most expensive automobiles in the world.

"Whoa, check out that car!" Felicity exclaimed, impressed. "It must be at least the governor visiting. I mean, who in this dump would be picked up by a sweet ride like that?"

At that moment, Zachary slipped out from behind the wheel and surveyed the milling students. At last, he recognized Jax and waved. "Nice to see you again, Mr. Jack." He opened the rear door and stood waiting for his passenger.

Jax felt the heat from his face crisping the air around him.

Felicity gaped. "You've got a *limo*?"

"It isn't mine," Jax said quickly. "It's my — dentist's. They offer pick-up service."

She looked at him in disbelief. "I must be going to the wrong dentist."

Jax rushed into the car before he could be caught in any more obvious lies. "Listen, Zachary, from now on do you think you can park a couple of blocks away? The Bentley kind of stands out."

"Certainly, Mr. Jack. From now on, I'll stop in front of the mortuary, where a limousine won't look quite so out of place."

The drive to the Quackenbush estate took half an hour, long enough for Jax to enjoy a few snacks from the minibar. Eating kept his mind off the job that lay ahead — keeping a dying man alive by a technique that had never been tested, using a power Jax himself still didn't fully understand.

All that Opus and Sparks hoopla had better be true or I'll have one very ticked-off billionaire on my hands!

Avery Quackenbush received Jax in a palatial sitting room just off the master bedroom. Instead of the usual nurses, he was accompanied by a bald man in a business suit and white lab coat.

The billionaire performed the introduction. "Say hello to Dr. Pavel. He's a big pain in my neck, and you probably won't like him either. He's in a lousy mood most of the time because it's his responsibility to keep me from dropping dead, and that's not the easiest job in the world."

Dr. Pavel shook Jax's hand. "I want to tell you up front that I don't approve of this 'treatment.' What exactly are you planning to do to my patient?"

Jax was tongue-tied.

"Don't let this overpriced sawbones intimidate you," the tycoon prodded. "You're a master at what you do."

"I'm not really sure exactly how this is supposed to work," Jax admitted. "I'm going to hypnotize Mr.

Quackenbush and try to relax him. I guess the idea is that, over time, I might be able to slow down his metabolism."

"And the science behind this is . . . ?" the doctor prompted dubiously.

"A lot happens with the mind that science can't explain," Jax replied, a little annoyed at being criticized for something that hadn't even been his idea in the first place. "That doesn't make it magic or supernatural — it's just something we haven't figured out yet. . . ." His voice trailed off as he recognized where he'd gotten that explanation. It had come from Dr. Mako, his worst enemy.

"Good answer!" Quackenbush approved. "Now let's get on with it. I'm not getting any younger." To the doctor, he said, "Beat it, so the kid can do his thing."

"Of course I'll be staying to monitor your vital signs," Pavel sniffed.

"If I had vital signs, I wouldn't need either one of you!" the billionaire growled. "Oh, all right — but get in the way and you're out on your ear."

Eventually Jax and his subject faced each other across an elegant tooled-leather tabletop. Jax took a deep breath and peered into the tycoon's faded gray eyes. It was not a smooth hypnotism. A mesmeric link required submission, and Quackenbush was used to being in charge. It wasn't natural for him to submit.

"You are feeling drowsy," Jax suggested.

"Says you!" came the belligerent response.

Jax bore down, focusing his strength into his deep purple gaze. Maybe this frail old man was the alpha male in the boardroom, but when minds were wrestling for control, the advantage always went to the guy named Opus.

The PIP was very faint at first, and blotchy around the edges. As the detail filled in and Jax could see what his subject saw, he realized that the tycoon's vision was failing along with the rest of his body's functions. Jax's image of himself was indistinct, and the tubes and wires that were inside Quackenbush's field of vision were just a blur.

Jax was at a loss for a moment. This was the point when the mind-bender would give his subject a task to perform or implant a post-hypnotic suggestion to be triggered at a later time. In this case, though, the goal was less specific. He could not order a person to slow his heart rate or reduce his metabolism. If that were true, hypnotists would be medical magicians, commanding broken bones to heal and damaged organs to repair themselves. The only way he had half a chance of helping Avery Quackenbush was by relaxing him.

"You are very calm and tranquil," he said, feeling like a novice hypnotist on his first day at Sentia. One of Mako's favorite lectures was that there were infinite ways to bring a subject to a desired state.

"You're floating on a cloud, weightless, boneless, and free of any care in the world. Gravity has no hold on you; nothing pulls you down. You feel total satisfaction, happiness, even joy. . . ."

Out of the corner of his eye, he caught sight of Dr. Pavel checking monitors and readouts. It would have been helpful to know what these indicated, but he dared not let his attention wander, for fear of weakening the mesmeric link.

He tried a few other descriptive scenarios — lying on feather beds, drifting on a gentle current, swaying to soft, beautiful music. At one point, he was aware of the doctor taking his patient's heart rate and whispering, "Remarkable!" Jax couldn't be sure exactly what that meant, but it sounded encouraging. He was really too tired to think about it much. A yawn escaped him. It was hard to come here after a full day of school, when he was just so sleepy. . . .

He sat bolt upright, suddenly aware of what was happening to him. This wasn't *his* drowsiness — it was Quackenbush's! With a flicker of one eye, he checked the antique grandfather clock over the tycoon's shoulder and realized in shock that the mesmeric link was nearly half an hour old. It hadn't seemed anywhere near that long. Mindbenders frequently implanted post-hypnotic suggestions to be activated days or even weeks later. But it was unusual to be connected to a subject for more than a few minutes. Anything longer than that left the hypnotist's mind exposed. And now Quackenbush's relaxation was beginning to leach into Jax.

Jax tensed his body in the hope that physical alertness would extend to his mind. But a moment later, he heard the doctor murmur, "Heart rate rising . . ."

I can't wake myself up without doing the same to Mr. Quackenbush!

There was no choice but to sink back into this stupor and just hang on.

He might have dozed off if it hadn't been for the ache in both knees. It traveled up his legs into his hips and across his lower back. Stiffness, too, the kind that came from sitting too long in one place. And his neck, his shoulders —

It's not my pain! It's his!

This was what it felt like to be ninety-six and dying! And Jax was picking it up through the pain center in his subject's mind.

With a sense of dread, Jax realized that he was entering completely uncharted territory here. Even at Sentia, no one had ever stayed linked for this long. Where would this end? He was plagued by nightmare thoughts straight out of horror movies about brain transfers. There he'd be, trapped inside a wasted ancient wreck of a body while Quackenbush fled the scene in a stolen twelve-year-old model, scarcely used. What if this had been the tycoon's plan all along? In a long life filled with successful business deals, surely this would count as the greatest transaction of them all!

Bail out of this!

Every fiber of his being screamed at him to break the connection, to escape while he still could. But what about the money — what about Mom and Dad and the life they'd never have again without it? And what about Avery Quackenbush, who was fighting for his life? Jax had made him a promise. Surely that had to count for something.

"You are very calm," he mumbled aloud again, although this time the message was intended for himself.

Somehow, he had to find a safe place between zoning out and freaking out.

The session was approaching the one-hour point when he finally made it. It wasn't comfort exactly, but even pain and misery became the new normal if you were stuck with them long enough. He crawled into an alcove in his mind and huddled there, enduring. This had to be over soon, although no one had ever talked about the timing of it. He hoped he'd know when the moment was right.

And then a bullet whizzed by his right ear.

The gate before him crashed down and Jax was carried forward in a crush of men — armed men, weighed down with helmets and heavy equipment. A moment later, he was over his waist in icy water, pounding through the surf.

Am I hallucinating?

He wanted to ask the soldier beside him, but the man was dead, bleeding from a wound in his chest, right next to his grenade.

Grenade?

Jax looked down at the object he was gripping so tightly with both hands, holding it high, above the waves. It was a rifle.

All along the beach, soldiers exactly like him were splashing toward the safety of the shore. No — not safety. They were taking withering fire. Bodies dropped. White water churned pink with blood.

A shell burst overhead and he landed face-first in the surf, choking on sand and salt. He came up gasping and spitting, his heart pounding with fear. But it was not Jackson Opus's fear at this hallucination. Because this was no hallucination. It was Avery Quackenbush's real memories of landing on Omaha Beach in the World War II D-Day invasion.

That's impossible! Jax thought frantically. *This can't be just a memory! No memory feels this real.*

Braintree's words came to him: *The mind you'll be entering is a museum housing nearly a century of memories and experiences. . . . Your twelve years of life cannot possibly prepare you for the onslaught. . . .*

Off to the left, an unfortunate landing craft struck a bobbing mine. The amphibious vehicle exploded in a geyser of water and flame. Jax could see bodies flung clear, along with the debris. A fragment of shrapnel glanced off his helmet, stunning him momentarily. If its path had been a few inches lower, it would have killed him.

He might have stood there, overwhelmed by terror and sheer sensory input, if the waves of men behind him hadn't pushed him forward onto the beach. Here the whine of incoming bullets was like an attack of enraged mosquitoes — deadly ones. Soldiers were dropping all around, alive one moment, gone the next, often without a sound. The living flopped down right along with the dead, in an attempt to stay under the barrage. Boot camp had taught them to slither on their bellies, and Jax did that now, inching ever forward. It was pure horror — crawling not just over sand but also over your dead companions. In an instant, he understood how this memory of seventy years ago could be so present and so alive. This experience could not be taken in all at once. It could only be compartmentalized — filed away to be dealt with in bits and pieces small enough to be processed and understood. Avery Quackenbush had been reliving this ever since the actual D-Day. And now Jax was reliving it through his mesmeric link with the old soldier.

To Jax's amazement, his sudden realization of what he was living through did nothing to lessen his panic. He could not be killed here because he was not actually here. Even Quackenbush obviously did not die on Omaha Beach because he was still alive seventy years afterward. Yet the terror that he felt belonged to Corporal Quackenbush in the heat of battle, primal and gut-wrenching and real. He clambered up and over a barrier made of loose rock, ducking under a line of iron "hedgehogs," huge obstacles that resembled gigantic metal jacks. Beside him, a tank struggled against one of these, unable to move it or pass over it. As Jax watched, a caterpillar track was ripped clean off the armored vehicle, leaving it an easy target for the barrage coming from the bluff some two hundred yards ahead.

At this point, the mission became appallingly clear. Hundreds — thousands — of American infantry scrambled across the beach toward the base of the escarpment. They were expected to make it up the steep slope with German snipers shooting down at them from fortified pillboxes and artillery casements.

It can't be done! They'll pick us off, one at a time!

But as he reached the bottom and began to climb, he understood that the choice of whether or not to go on was not his. That decision had been made by Corporal

Quackenbush a long time ago. Jax could not imagine such courage, but he felt it pulsing through his veins.

His fear had already rendered him breathless; now the climb took away what little wind he had left. He made his painstaking way handhold by foothold, his rifle slung over his shoulder. If he needed it at an instant's notice — well, that would be too bad, wouldn't it? As it was, the invading GIs were hopelessly outgunned by the enemy soldiers in the pillbox above them — heavy machine guns firing down, ripping holes in the terrain all around.

We're sitting ducks!

His sergeant appeared at his shoulder, shouting over the din of battle. "If we can get past that pillbox —"

The man never got to finish his thought. A stray bullet ricocheted off a rock in front of them and struck him in the throat. He was gone even before he collapsed.

Now leaderless, the small company hunkered down behind their sergeant's body. There was grief, anger, panic, and every emotion in between. Jax heard none of it. In an almost trancelike state, he got to his feet and made a bull run at the pillbox, bent double against the slope. Bullets hailed all around, but miraculously none of them found him. He was now close enough to make out the muzzle of the machine gun protruding from the narrow slit in the concrete bunker. Leaving his feet in a desperation dive, he hit the ground and rolled up against the base of the pillbox. He took a grenade from his belt, and pulled the pin.

One . . . two . . . three . . .

He reached up and shoved it inside through the opening. Hunkering down, he held on to his helmet and prayed.

He felt the walls of the pillbox and the very ground itself jump. Strangely, though, he didn't hear the boom of the explosion, just a dull *thump*. The machine gun fell silent. Barely daring to breathe, he raised his head and peeked inside the concrete bunker.

The scream torn from his throat was barely human.

Jax came awake, still crying out in horror, to find Dr. Pavel shaking him by the shoulders. "Snap out of it! You're all right!"

"I killed them!" Jax wailed.

"No one is dead." The doctor's tone was insistent, yet soothing.

"But . . ." How could he explain what he'd seen inside that pillbox? Death, yes, but so much more. The merciless science of an exploding grenade in a confined space. It was impossible to recognize that the remains had been people just a few minutes before.

"You're in Avery Quackenbush's residence," the doctor informed him, "and you're perfectly fine."

Jax took stock of himself. He was in a cold sweat, trembling, his heartbeat rapid and shallow. But Omaha Beach was thousands of miles and seventy years away. He was in the sitting room, opposite the slumbering billionaire.

Slowly, he began to get himself under control. "How long . . . ?"

"Close to an hour and a half," Pavel replied.

"And I've been screaming all that time?"

"No, but something's been going on for the past half hour." The doctor indicated the tycoon's forest of monitor wires and IV tubes. "I was beginning to wonder if I'd have to order up a second set for *you*. What happened?"

"It's hard to explain." Dr. Pavel already knew that Jax was a mind-bender, so there was no secret to keep. But he didn't feel comfortable discussing his power with a medical man, who might bring up the subject with colleagues. Any buzz about a boy hypnotist could get back to Mako. "It's a side effect of the mesmeric link. I got too far into his head. I hope it didn't upset Mr. Quackenbush."

"On the contrary, you succeeded in putting him into a deep, relaxing sleep. His vital signs are stable. I can't say for sure what you've done to yourself in the process."

"No, it's good news," Jax countered. "This is why he hired me in the first place. To slow down his metabolism to keep him alive until the new treatment is ready."

Dr. Pavel's expression was skeptical. "I told him it was a faint hope. There is no medical evidence about this so-called human hibernation."

"But it's still worth a try, right?" Jax persisted. "I mean, if he's going to die anyway, he's got nothing to lose."

"*He's* got nothing to lose," Pavel agreed. "*You*, on the other hand, are a healthy twelve-year-old with your whole life ahead of you. I watched you. Respiration and heart rate elevated, probably your blood pressure, too. Extreme emotional disturbance with the possibility of post-traumatic stress. If I were *your* doctor and not Mr. Quackenbush's, I'd recommend that you never try this again."

12

Axel Braintree had a way of keeping his ankles limber by gripping his toes and rotating his feet, first clockwise, then counterclockwise, a hundred times in each direction. He did it sitting on the edge of his bed, which shook the bed itself, the attic floor, and the entire house. Added to this sound was the noise of Jax's mother banging a broom against the ceiling. Of all the old hypnotist's habits, she found this one the most infuriating.

"Fascinating!" he exclaimed without a break in the foot-rhythm. "I read years ago that Quackenbush won a Silver Star in the war. It must have been for that very incident. And you *lived* it!"

"It was horrible!" Jax complained. "I killed three people — blew them to bits!"

"*You* didn't. Quackenbush did."

"But it *felt* like me," Jax practically moaned. "And even though it's over, I still have the guilt. I don't know how he lives with it."

"There was a war on," Braintree reminded him. "'Kill or be killed' is a very strong incentive, and that applied not just to soldiers, but entire countries. When Quackenbush looked inside that pillbox — as awful as it was — he saw a necessary piece of a much larger puzzle. But without the big picture of a world at war, you saw only a hideous massacre. I warned you that this was the risk of opening yourself up to the memories and experiences of someone who had lived so long and done so much."

"What I can't figure out," Jax wondered, "is how was *he* so relaxed? Wouldn't he have to be reliving the same memory I was trapped in?"

Braintree switched ankles. "There's no textbook on this, Jax. Just as your remote hypnotism was unique in the world, you are breaking new ground with this extended mesmeric connection. In a brief, shallow link you pick up current thoughts and impressions. But a longer exposure can take you on a journey anywhere inside your subject's mind. And all the while, Mr. Quackenbush is relaxing as you've instructed him. Although your minds are joined, you have gone your separate ways."

"So how do I protect myself tomorrow?" Jax asked anxiously.

The pounding resumed from downstairs.

Braintree let go of his foot and stood up. "Has your mother bought a new meat tenderizer?"

"What? No. I mean, I don't think so."

The old man shuffled into his slippers. "Well, I'm glad we had this little chat. . . ."

"That's it?" Jax was irritated. "Axel, are you even listening to me?"

Braintree shook his head. "I'm sorry, Jax. I have to

confess I'm a little distracted tonight. I'm concerned that something might be happening with my sandmen. No one has seen Evelyn in weeks. I told Ivan it was probably a coincidence, but now I can't reach him either."

"Well . . ." Jax didn't want to appear too critical of the guild members. Braintree had a fatherly view of his flock of New York–area hypnotists, despite the legal scrapes their special talent always managed to get them into. "I mean, it wouldn't be the first time one of the sandmen had to lie low for a while."

"Yes, *one* of the sandmen," Axel agreed. "Not two. And when Elias Mako is out for revenge. He knows that I'm helping you and he knows my connection to the guild. But that's my problem, not yours. What was your question?"

"How do I keep myself from getting sucked into Quackenbush's memories?" asked Jax, feeling a little selfish to be focusing on his own problems at a moment when the sandmen could be in trouble.

"I fear that it can't be avoided," the old man told him. "Mr. Quackenbush is asking for a deep and intense mesmeric connection. It stands to reason that the side effects will also be deep and intense. In fact, in future sessions, you'll probably find that you'll slip into his memories more quickly each time, now that the hypnotic pathway has been opened."

In other words, Jax reflected glumly, *all I have to look forward to is more of the same.*

The reflection that peered back at Jax from the surface of the lake was completely unrecognizable. Seventeen-year-old Avery Quackenbush looked nothing like the ancient, shriveled figure encircled by tubes and wires in the high-tech wheelchair opposite Jax. The face on the surface of the water was rugged, with a strong jaw framing an expression of equal parts determination and confidence. It was almost as if the young Quackenbush could see the fabulously successful businessman he would one day become. Certainly, there was no sign of it in his current life — a high-school dropout struggling to help his mother make ends meet at the height of the Great Depression.

Jax never learned these details; it was more like he knew them already. Just as a new computer or phone came pre-loaded with software, he went on his mind-trips through the billionaire's life equipped with the knowledge and memories of the Avery Quackenbush of that moment. For example, he recognized the handsome teenager perched in the bow of the ancient wooden rowboat as his brother, Oscar — two years his junior. And he instantly understood that the impish grin on Oscar's features irritated him to no end. Didn't he see there was nothing to smile about? Their father was hundreds of miles away, looking for work. They were poor and perpetually hungry. Even those lucky few with money found little to spend it on. Years of drought had turned most of the country into a great dust bowl. Although Jax's stomach was full, he could feel the gnawing emptiness of his subject's belly that afternoon in 1934.

"Take us out to the deepest water," Oscar ordered. "If you want the biggest fish, you have to go where they are."

"There haven't been fish in this pond for two years," Jax heard himself retort. These days, if it could be cooked and eaten, it was probably already gone. People who were hungry added to their food supply however they could. There were hardly any birds or squirrels either. Only the rats had been able to hold out. So far.

But he rowed to the center of the lake because Oscar always got his way. This was not Jax's thought — he had never even met Oscar Quackenbush. Yet he was aware of himself thinking it via the older brother's mind.

It was Jax's second mesmeric session with the billionaire, and he had accessed his subject's memories much more quickly, just as Braintree had predicted. He was *in character* — almost as if he were the starring actor in *The Avery Quackenbush Story*, coming soon to a theater near you. A new medical man — Dr. Finnerty — stood over the wheelchair monitoring the patient's vital signs today. Dr. Pavel was nowhere to be seen, and no one had answered Jax's question about where he was. Jax thought back to

Pavel's statement from yesterday: *If I were* your *doctor and not Mr. Quackenbush's, I'd recommend that you never try this again.* Apparently, now he wasn't the billionaire's doctor either. That seemed to be the price of telling the famous tycoon what he didn't want to hear.

The brothers' fishing poles were homemade — tree branches, string, bent safety pins as hooks. Bait was stale bread because Oscar was too squeamish to use worms. Jax wasn't sure just how long they sat in the boat, getting not so much as a nibble. It was probably hours, but luckily, Quackenbush's memory edited out the boring parts. All at once, Oscar threw down his pole and leaped to his feet, causing the craft to rock dangerously.

"Move us forward!" Oscar yelled. "Quick!"

"Sit down, idiot!" Jax snapped. "Unless you feel like swimming!"

Oscar snatched up their "net" — a length of old lace curtains. "Hurry! There's a whopper over there!"

"Sit down, I told you," Jax said irritably. "I'm not capsizing us so you can chase some old boot —"

And then he saw it, just below the surface — a long silver body, the great-granddaddy of all trout. "Don't lose him! If he's survived this long, it's because he's wily! Give me the net!"

"In a pig's eye! He's mine!" Grasping the curtain with both hands, Oscar made a low scooping motion through the water and missed.

"He's nobody's if you let him get away!" Jax could feel Quackenbush's excitement. He had not expected this fishing trip to bear fruit. But now the possibility of bringing something home to Mother for the dinner table had acquired a desperate urgency. It would be nice to see her smile again. He couldn't remember the last time that had happened. . . .

Oscar took another swipe, deeper this time. For a moment the trout was in his net, all sixteen inches of it, flopping and fighting for its life. The effort to hold on sent the boy staggering across the flat-bottom craft. He tripped on his abandoned fishing pole and somersaulted over the side, whacking his head on the gunwale as he fell. He sank like a stone, leaving a trail of bubbles in his wake.

In an instant, the picture of Mother's grateful smile vanished. Coming home fishless was one thing; coming home Oscar-less was quite another. Without even kicking off his shoes, he jumped out of the boat in search of his rash young brother. The lake was ice cold, which made his heart race. But his biggest concern was that the water was dark and murky, and he couldn't see a thing. Panic rose in his throat. How was he ever going to find Oscar?

His lungs burned from lack of oxygen. He kicked for the surface, took a great gulp of air, and dove again, the water stinging his eyes as he flailed his arms in the hope of encountering his brother. The sickening *crunch* of Oscar's head hitting the wooden gunwale still rang in his ears. If the blow had knocked him unconscious, he was probably already at the bottom of this deep lake.

"Wake up!" came a voice that rang with alarm.

"I have to save Oscar —"

"Wake up and wake *him* up, too!" This was punctuated by a sharp slap across Jax's face.

He came to himself with a start to find Dr. Finnerty shaking him by the shoulders. The two nurses were also there, leaning over their patient.

"What's happening?" Jax blurted.

"He's having heart palpitations," the doctor explained briskly. "I don't want to treat him until I'm sure he's free of whatever trance you've put him in."

Jax approached the billionaire and intoned, "When I snap my fingers, you'll come back to yourself, feeling refreshed and happy, and breathing deeply —"

"Don't worry about the details," Dr. Finnerty cut in. "Just wake him. Now."

Jax snapped his fingers and Quackenbush opened his eyes. But before he could say anything, the doctor injected a small syringe of liquid into his IV tube, and his eyes closed again.

Jax hung back, waiting, as the three medical people worked on his subject. Forty-five minutes later, Dr. Finnerty escorted him in to speak to the billionaire, who was resting comfortably in his bed.

"Was it my fault?" Jax whispered to the doctor. "Was it something I did?"

Dr. Finnerty shrugged. "I don't presume to understand what you do."

The billionaire overheard and emitted a snort of disgust. "Don't tell the kid that — he'll blame himself! It's my bum ticker, which works about as well as everything else I've got. This kind of thing happens every time the wind blows — it's part of the Catastrophic Systemic Shutdown."

"Yeah, but I'm supposed to make things better, not worse," Jax said ruefully.

"There's no medical evidence," put in Dr. Finnerty, "that you can make things either better *or* worse."

"Another county heard from," snarled Quackenbush. "You know, you wouldn't be the first doctor I fired this week."

Mystery solved: Dr. Pavel got the boot.

"I'm just pointing out," Finnerty said, "that I'm here to look after your physical health, but any paranormal activity is beyond my ability and experience. I couldn't even begin to guess what happens when you two are 'connected.' "

"Yeah, I'm kind of curious about that, too." Quackenbush turned his sharp eyes to Jax. "What's it like inside this old head? Any cobwebs? Stalactites? Tow-away zones?"

Jax smiled timidly. "I get caught up in your memories."

The billionaire's face clouded. "You can read my mind?"

"It's not something I'm *doing*," Jax tried to explain. "It just happens. When you hypnotize somebody, there's a link between you. Normally, it doesn't go very far, because you can plant a suggestion and get out pretty fast. But with you, I have to stay connected for a long time, and your mind washes back into mine. It starts off with just feelings and impressions, but eventually I end up inside your memories."

Quackenbush propped himself against his pillows and folded his arms in front of him. "Like what?"

Jax took a deep breath. "Like Normandy. When you went up the bluff and took out that enemy pillbox."

The old soldier raised bushy eyebrows. "I never tell anybody about that."

"You didn't tell me either," Jax tried to explain. "I was inside your memory. In a way, it became *my* memory. When I think back on it, it's like it happened to me."

"Well, you can keep it," Quackenbush grumbled. "I've been trying to forget it every day since. Maybe that's why it came up — because I've been subconsciously looking for somebody to take it off my hands. What else did you dig out of my head?"

"You and Oscar were fishing on a lake," Jax supplied, "and Oscar went overboard. You jumped in to rescue him, and that's when Dr. Finnerty woke me up." He hesitated. "Did you save him? What happened?"

The tycoon laughed out loud. "Of course I saved him. That was my life's purpose — pulling that fool out of some jackpot. But you know what?" His faded eyes twinkled with the memory. "When I heaved him back into the boat, damned if he didn't have that trout clutched in his arms like a football. We had a real feed that night, let me tell you!"

"Interesting," Dr. Finnerty put in. "I understand why D-Day came up so readily. It was one of the most important dates of the last century. But two brothers on a fishing trip?"

"I thought you were only interested in the medical side of this," Quackenbush growled.

"There's a psychological component to medicine," the doctor reasoned. "Something in your relationship with your brother puts this simple memory on a par with the invasion of Europe. Were you and Oscar very close?"

All at once, the pale features became suffused with purple. "I'm not paying good money to have my head shrunk by the likes of you!"

The heart monitor began to beep.

"Clear the room," Dr. Finnerty ordered.

Quackenbush was still sputtering, the veins pulsing in his temples. "I can't keep the kid out of my head, but you're not invited!"

"This isn't helping, Mr. Quackenbush. Try to calm yourself."

"I'll be calm when you stop minding my business!"

A nurse tried to hurry Jax out of the room. He shrugged her off and fixed his dark, serious gaze on the billionaire. "When I clap my hands, you will remember nothing of this conversation, just that you are relaxed and in a pleasant mood. . . ."

Behind him, he distinctly heard the doctor whisper, "There's a first time for everything."

The return had not been planned.

Axel Braintree hadn't been to New York since going into hiding with the Opuses. But the disappearances of Evelyn Lolis and Ivan Marcinko had brought him out of hiding. He had purchased a prepaid throwaway cell phone and gotten in touch with Dennison Cho. He'd heard nothing for two hours, and then his throwaway unit rang. It was Cho calling from the 78th Precinct in Brooklyn, under arrest on misdemeanor fraud charges — selling paper cups filled with dirt to hypnotized customers who thought they were purchasing exotic orchids. He'd been given one phone call. This was it.

As Braintree came up out of the subway, the sights and smells of the city brought him something like joy. Oh, how he missed this place! There was something about the heartbeat of New York that was in sync with his own. He was not meant for Connecticut, with its open spaces and strip malls.

Today's trip, though, was strictly business. At the precinct house, Braintree posted the bail and led Cho out into a nearby park.

"I hope you've learned your lesson, Dennison," Braintree scolded. "We have a gift, but the greatest gift is the willpower not to use it. No amount of hypnotism can change the fact that crime doesn't pay."

"That was just rotten luck," the arrestee explained. "Some satisfied customer was so delighted with his orchid that he had to show it off — to a cop!"

The old man sighed. "Well, at least you weren't foolish enough to try to bend the police officer."

"Oh, I did," Cho explained cheerfully. "But a funny thing happened. Before I could get into his head, I got the feeling that somebody was working his way into mine."

Braintree was instantly alert. "Someone tried to hypnotize you?"

"I thought it might be the officer at first. But no, the power wasn't coming from him."

"Who, then?"

"I never saw who it was," the arrestee admitted with a shrug. "The cop was in a real hurry to cuff me and hustle me into the squad car — you know, get another menace to society off the street."

Braintree rolled his eyes. "Listen to me, Dennison, and listen well. Evelyn and Ivan have both gone missing. I believe that someone is kidnapping sandmen, and you were about to be next, except that your arrest got in the way."

Cho looked vaguely pleased. "But who's doing it? And why?"

Braintree thought it over. Mako was the obvious enemy, but his target was Jax, not the sandmen. What did he need hypnotists for when he already headed an entire institute full of them? Of course, Mako couldn't be the only power-mad thug who saw the value of an army of mind-benders. What about Avery Quackenbush? The billionaire was wealthy enough to impose his will any way he chose. What if his illness was just a sham so he could get his hands on an Opus? Maybe he was after even more hypnotists.

"It's too early to tell," Braintree said finally. "The important thing is to be careful. And spread the word to the other sandmen. They're in danger, too. We all are."

The locomotive was big and shiny black. It lumbered around the oval track, pulling a coal car, a flat car, and a red caboose. The hum of the electric motor added to the sounds of metal wheels on metal track. As Jax watched it through the billionaire's memory, he could tell that it was the most wonderful thing nine-year-old Avery Quackenbush had ever laid eyes on.

Father said it was called a starter set. More track could be purchased, trestles built, stations added. There were boxcars, passenger coaches, and Pullmans, where tiny seats turned into beds.

As the details of the memory became more vivid via the mesmeric link, Jax took in the frost on the windows, the tantalizing cooking smells coming from the kitchen, and the gleaming tinsel and ornaments on the tree. It was Christmas morning, he realized. No, it was the greatest Christmas morning ever, which was really saying something from the perspective of someone who had experienced nearly a hundred of them. Jax, who lived in a house filled with computers, game systems, and smartphones, could almost taste young Avery's amazement and delight at this toy that lit up and moved like a real train.

Through the mind of the nine-year-old, Jax understood that times were good. Father was doing well at his job, and the family had money to lavish presents on its two children. In the moment of that memory, Jax could detect no knowledge that, a handful of years from now, the world would be sunk into depression, and the Quackenbush brothers would be desperate to catch a fish so they and their mother wouldn't starve.

"It's not fair!"

Jax frowned. Oscar, age seven, had decided to be jealous of the Lionel train set. Never mind that he had received an entire Civil War battlefield — soldiers and cannons and horses and all the trimmings. It was another starter set that could be built into a lifelong hobby.

Oscar loved it. At least, he *had* loved it until he'd seen the locomotive chug off down the electrified track. His soldiers had to be moved by hand, but this ran by itself.

"Go play with your own present!" Jax heard himself snap.

And Oscar did, adjusting the fixed bayonet at the end of a tiny rifle. But the instant Father went into the kitchen to help Mother, Oscar sprang into action. That was another thing about Oscar. He didn't think; he *did*.

He snatched up the locomotive in mid-chug, shaking off the other cars from their hooked connectors. Then, shiny black engine in hand, he raced for the basement stairs.

"You rotten little —" Jax leaped up in pursuit. In full panic mode, he raced after his brother. "Don't you dare!"

Too late. He reached the landing just as Oscar let fly with all the pent-up rage of his jealousy. Jax watched his cherished locomotive go. He wasn't sure if young Avery knew about slow motion in 1926, but that was how Jax saw it — slo-mo, end over end. It crashed to the cement floor and flew apart, pins, nuts, bolts, wheels, and moving pieces scattering in all directions.

Avery's fury blinded Jax then. Without even knowing what he was doing, he took hold of his younger brother under the arms and began to force him toward the stairs. Terrified, Oscar sunk his teeth into Jax's forearm. There was sharp pain, and blood, but no reduction in Jax's determination to leave Oscar at the bottom of the stairs, in as broken a condition as the Lionel train.

"Avery! Avery, stop it!" Suddenly Father was on the scene, his powerful arms wresting Oscar from Jax's control.

As the basement staircase faded along with the mesmeric connection, Jax understood at last why this domestic scene of Christmas morning had created such a powerful memory even so many years later.

If Father hadn't come, I would have done it, he thought. *It's* Avery *who would have done it,* he amended as he disengaged fully and took stock of himself in his chair opposite the billionaire. He might have crippled or even killed his own brother over a toy.

Quackenbush was watching him curiously. "Okay, out with it. Which part of the magical mystery tour did you take this time?"

Jax flushed. "Christmas. The train set."

Quackenbush nodded thoughtfully. "What determines that? Are you — browsing my brain?"

"I have no control over where I end up," Jax tried to explain. "But it seems like the biggest memories are the ones that bubble up to the surface and pull me in. Like D-Day. And I think maybe this one was important because . . ." He hesitated. "Because this was the day you might have killed your brother."

Jax waited in trepidation. It was a very bold thing to say. But after all, this was no intrusion. Quackenbush had invited him in.

The tycoon was expressionless for a moment. Jax could imagine what it must have been like to face him across a boardroom table.

The billionaire let out a melancholy sigh. "My father, in his infinite wisdom, came up with a way to punish Oscar for breaking my train. You know what it was? He gave me the Civil War battlefield. I put it back in the crate, and as far as I know, it's still there, untouched."

Jax ran his mind over the memory — the murderous impulse to fling a helpless seven-year-old down the stairs.

It wasn't the kind of thing you could shut away in a box.

Keeping a low profile at Haywood Middle School was getting harder every day. Maybe it was the sunglasses, or the sightings around town of Jax climbing into the Quackenbush limo. The chess championship didn't help, especially since Mr. Isaacs seemed to have a vivid memory of how brilliant Jax had been in the tournament that had never happened at all. Jax was honored at an assembly, and his picture was placed on the school's Wall of Fame. They made him take off his sunglasses for that photograph, and there always seemed to be a few people around the bulletin board, just standing and staring.

That was how Jack Magnus became the first middle-school student ever to be caught defacing his own picture. He blacked out his eyes, and drew a goatee and a curly mustache. This only seemed to add to his legend.

"You're even too cool for the things that make you look cool," Felicity told him.

"I don't understand it," he complained to Braintree. "I'm not hypnotizing anybody, but I'm still getting all this attention!"

As usual, the founder of the Sandman's Guild had an

explanation. "A weapon doesn't have to be fired in order for it to have power. It influences the world around it merely when it is wielded. You don't have to bend anyone for your hypnotic presence to assert itself. There's an aura about you that sunglasses can never completely conceal."

Jax looked worried. It had happened in New York, too, where he had been elected to student council without running, and had enjoyed a popularity that had eclipsed his best friend, Tommy, for no real reason. The difference was that, in New York, the entire family's fate hadn't hung on Jax's ability to disappear.

"So what do I do? How do I fade into the background again?"

"You'll have to find a way."

It was not the kind of specific game plan Jax had been hoping for. Normally, Braintree was a treasure trove of mesmeric information: Cat owners were harder to bend than dog owners. . . . It was possible to affect someone's driving by placing a hypnotic image in his rearview mirror (a charging rhino would speed him up; a police car would slow him down). . . . You couldn't mesmerize someone to fall in love, but you could make sure he always remembered where he'd left the TV remote. . . . Babies could be hypnotized (the trick was to communicate to them what you wanted them to do). . . . It went on and on.

Lately, though, the old man's mind had been in New York with his sandmen. And while it was a relief not to be quizzed constantly on which Opus bent Benedict Arnold to turn into a traitor, there was a flip side to this new, distracted Braintree.

Jax's main source of support wasn't quite there anymore.

Jax continued to visit the mansion every weekday after school. His hypnotic sessions with the billionaire grew increasingly intense as the two minds became more accustomed to each other. The connection was always stressful for Jax. He struggled to maintain his own sense of self as he was drawn into the life of another, thinking and experiencing a strange world as someone else. At times it was hard to get a handle on where the billionaire's thoughts ended and his own began.

The memories stretched through most of the twentieth century into the twenty-first. In 1929, the Quackenbush siblings traced a path through downtown streets around long lines of panicked depositors, frantic to get into banks and withdraw money while there was still money to withdraw. Jax relived the brothers' horror at turning a corner and finding the broken body of a stockbroker who had just jumped from a high window. During the Great Depression that followed, the ever-present hunger of an empty belly and the gnawing fear for the future became Jax's own. And the horrible war memories — unimaginable death and destruction, all-pervading chaos, crawling on his belly through filth and gore, lethal bullets passing inches above his helmet.

Jax experienced the billionaire's business career, too — huge risks, stratospheric celebration, bitter disappointment. There were ruthless dealings that left opponents and competitors not just outmaneuvered, but utterly destroyed.

In one crushingly vivid memory, he watched a business rival bankrupted so completely that his family was evicted from their home in the middle of the night. Rising titan Avery Quackenbush had observed from his car, parked at the curb, while the man's weeping wife and children were removed from the premises by the sheriff. As Jax peered out the car window, the clash of the billionaire's brutal satisfaction and Jax's own sympathy and guilt nearly tore him in two. The way Quackenbush had attacked that machine-gun pillbox on Omaha Beach was identical to the way he approached everything in life — all out, and with no mercy.

A man like that made many enemies, but Jax only encountered one directly. He was stepping from his limousine and walking toward the lobby of Quackenbush Tower in London when a conservatively dressed man in a bowler hat stepped out of a red telephone booth, pulling a pistol from his jacket. The impact of the bullet reminded Jax of being struck with a flying pebble kicked up by a passing car. It hurt a lot less than the onslaught of flying bodyguards who lifted him up and jammed him into the safety of the revolving door, imprisoning him. He hung there, stunned, while his protectors chased down the assassin and held him for the police.

It was only then that Jax looked down and realized that he was clutching his stomach and that dark red blood was seeping through his fingers. The pain came then, white-hot and overwhelming. He was barely conscious by the time the ambulance arrived.

The most amazing thing about it was that Jax was aware of pain and fear, but surprisingly little anger at the would-be assassin.

"That's the cost of doing business," the billionaire told him after the session was over. "I ruined him, he shot me. I suppose I could have sued for damages, but I already had most of his money, so what would be the point? I didn't even testify at the trial. The last thing I needed was another trip to England so I could order chips and get fries."

Quackenbush was peculiar in many ways. He fought hard for his wealth and social position, and then used it mostly to ignore people. He avoided parties, and never hosted any of his own unless there was some business advantage to be gained. He employed several chefs, but preferred a hamburger or a grilled-cheese sandwich to any gourmet dish they could come up with. He never married, had no children, and didn't question if he was missing something. He owned a major-league baseball team and had never attended one of their games, not even when they won the World Series. They were simply an investment, like Apple or AT&T.

Some of the experiences were upsetting simply because Jax, at twelve, had never been through anything like them — Quackenbush's mother's funeral in 1969, or his 1985 heart attack, a sensation that felt like his chest was being sucked out of his body by a titanic Shop-Vac.

There was no chronological order to the memories. One afternoon he might be in his eighties, receiving an award from the grand duke of Luxembourg, or pulling off a coup that netted a hundred million dollars in a single afternoon. The next, he would be back in the Depression as a teenager. Most of the childhood memories involved Oscar. In spite of their fighting, the Quackenbush brothers had apparently been inseparable.

"Is Oscar still living?" Jax asked Quackenbush one day.

His response was a rueful snort. "*I'm* not still living, if you talk to any of these so-called medical men! When you get to my age, everybody's already in the ground. Wait till *my* funeral. They'll hold it in a phone booth."

So Oscar was dead. Jax shouldn't have been surprised. He would have been ninety-four. But Jax had only known him as a young boy so, against all logic, his death seemed untimely and tragic.

Jax mourned him.

Even Braintree had to admit that the damage was not small.

"Look what you've done to my car!" the woman wailed, pointing to the bashed-in door of her white BMW. "I just got it last week! It doesn't have a hundred miles on it!"

The sandman was trying to calm her. "Well, you know, my car doesn't look so good either. Look at the fender."

"Whose fault is that?" she shrilled. "They teach you in kindergarten that red means stop!"

Braintree felt a warm wet trickle under his nose. He looked down to see a droplet of blood decorate his white shirt front. "The important thing is no one was injured."

"Not yet!" she snapped back. "When my husband sees this car, he's going to pull your ponytail out through your belly button!"

He felt the old temptation rising. It would be so much simpler to bend her to believe that the car was in perfect condition, not even scratched. But how would he ever face the guild if he used hypnotism to take the easy way out here? He'd be a hypocrite. Worse, he'd lose all moral authority as the leader of his flock.

"Ma'am, please put your cell phone away. I'm sure we can come to a civilized agreement."

"Dave!" she barked into the handset. "You're never going to believe this! I was pulling out of the plaza, and some old geezer plowed into me!"

To make matters worse, his own cell phone rang — not his regular one, but the throwaway phone he used to make emergency calls to the sandmen.

He didn't recognize the incoming number. "Yes, yes, who is this?"

"Axel . . . Axel . . ." The voice was barely a whisper, full of panic. "Axel, it's me — Evelyn!"

Braintree was instantly breathless. "What happened to you? Are you safe?"

"They're after me!" Lolis rasped. "I've hurt my leg! I think my ankle's broken!"

"Where's Ivan?" Braintree persisted. "Who else is with you?" There was no way Evelyn could have this number unless she'd gotten it from one of the handful of sandmen Braintree had shared it with. That meant at least one more must have been kidnapped.

"I'm at the corner of Eighty-Ninth and Crummel in the Bronx — a big warehouse building with a water tower on top! I don't think I can make it on my own! I've been bent three ways to Sunday! Who knows what post-hypnotic suggestions they've planted in my head?"

"Who's bent you?" Braintree demanded, his voice rising. "Who's got you?"

But at that moment, the connection broke. He hit *69,

but received a message that the number was not in service.

"Dave says to wait with the cars until he gets here," the BMW lady informed him. "He's got a cop friend who's meeting us."

There were times, Braintree reflected sadly, that even the founder of the Sandman's Guild had to break the rules for the greater good. He could not risk getting hung up here when Evelyn needed his help. He stepped in front of the woman and gazed into her eyes. Although he knew this was absolutely necessary, he felt a deep sense of shame.

"You are standing beside a BMW that is in perfect condition. . . ."

"Did you have to wear those sunglasses in your school picture?"

"Yes, Mom," Jax replied wearily. "Because I didn't want to have to tell the photographer which button to press by hypnotic command."

She grimaced. "I still don't understand how your father can be so perfectly normal and have passed on this hocus-pocus to his son."

"I told you. It skips generations sometimes. And stop blaming Dad alone. I'm not only an Opus; I'm a Sparks, too."

Her lips got thinner. "Well, the jury is still out on that one. I never knew any relatives named Sparks."

"You should come up to the attic," Jax replied shortly. "Axel's got your family tree plotted all the way back to

Leonardo da Vinci. Ever wonder why Mona Lisa looks so mellow?"

"It's not just the sunglasses," Mrs. Opus went on with a frown. "Your cheeks are sunken, your skin is pasty, like you just got out of jail." She turned from the photograph to her son. "You're too skinny. And your eyes . . ." She glanced away quickly, wary of his power to hypnotize. "They're bloodshot, and there are bags under them the size of suitcases."

He checked his reflection in the hall mirror. She was right, of course, but what did she expect? He was at school all day, struggling to avoid the spotlight. He had even taken the extraordinary step of implanting post-hypnotic suggestions in kids who wouldn't stop staring at him: "You've got more important things to worry about than Jack Magnus. It's like the guy doesn't even exist." The plan had backfired. Now he had to keep one eye out for people who might plow him over in the hall because they simply didn't see him. A girl named Carissa was sent to the principal's office for insisting he was absent from a class when she was sitting three desks away from him.

He had no friends because he couldn't risk other people finding out who and what he was. Felicity was kind of nice, but she was more of a stalker than a companion. She was too nosy and, mostly, too smart. She already knew there was something up with him — nobody went to the dentist so often. Anyway, he had no time for her. There was his after-school job at the Quackenbush estate, where he was cramming ninety-six years of memories into his twelve-year-old skull — the mental equivalent of trying to fit fifty pounds of potato salad into a five-pound container. Then dinner, homework, and an hour of sandman training from Braintree. When that was done, he would fall into bed and sleep like the dead until it was time to wake up and start the rat race all over again.

So he was looking a little tired and stressed-out. Shocker.

Mom wasn't just nagging. She was genuinely worried. "I don't feel comfortable leaving you in this state."

"Come on, Mom, it's your first Saturday night out with Dad since we left the city. I'm not going to drop dead in the time it takes for you guys to have dinner and see a movie."

She would not be distracted. "Maybe you should give up this after-school thing. I think it's wearing you down."

"We've been through this already," Jax retorted, a little impatiently. "We're going to need the money going forward."

"Your father and I still work. Nothing is worth sacrificing your health."

There was the squeal of tires in the driveway, and the sound of running feet on the walk. The door was flung wide to reveal a manic and pink-faced Braintree, his white shirt splattered red with blood.

Jax was instantly alert. "Axel, what's wrong?"

"I'll tell you what's wrong," Mrs. Opus cut in from where she was standing by the window. "He wrecked his car. The whole fender's bashed in."

"You're bleeding!" Jax exclaimed.

"It's nothing." Braintree headed for the attic stairs. "I just have to — freshen up," he mumbled under his breath.

Mom checked her watch. "I'm going to be late. There's leftover Chinese food in the fridge." She paused at the door and hissed, *"Do not drive with that man!"*

Jax watched her out the door, and then scrambled up the stairs. "Axel, what's going on? Do you need to see a doctor?"

"Forget the accident." Braintree was in the bathroom, washing the crusted blood from his face. "God knows the other person has. I just heard from Evelyn Lolis."

"That's great — isn't it?"

Breathlessly, the old man filled Jax in on the strange call over the throwaway phone. "She was very nervous, and not making a lot of sense." He pulled off the stained shirt and buttoned himself into a fresh one. "I'm going to go into the city and help her."

"I'll go with you," Jax said immediately.

"Absolutely not!" Braintree exclaimed. "This could be a trap!"

"Then why are *you* going?" Jax challenged.

"Because she needs me. And I have reason to believe she's been in contact with at least one other kidnapped sandman. She wouldn't have had this phone number unless she'd gotten it from somebody else."

The Sandman's Guild resembled a comedy routine at times, with Braintree lecturing about honesty to his band of petty crooks who were never going to change. But his devotion to his hypnotists was ironclad and 100 percent noble. Whatever the old man had to face tonight, Jax was determined that he would not face it alone.

"Come on, Axel — they're my sandmen, too. They saved my life in New York. Let me return the favor."

"It's out of the question," Braintree said stubbornly. "You're too important to the future." He headed for the stairs.

Jax blocked his way. "You're not going without me."

"Step aside," the old man ordered.

"Forget it."

Braintree stood glaring at him, and Jax felt the first stirring of someone trying to climb into his head.

His mentor was *hypnotizing* him!

“Come on, Axel,” Jax said peevishly. “Cut it out!”

But Braintree continued his assault, determined to protect Jax from what might lie ahead.

There was only one way to fight back. He mustered the strength from the Opus and Sparks genes inside him, and unleashed his gaze, his pale blue eyes darkening by the second.

Braintree blinked, taken aback by the strength of the counterattack. Then he ramped up his own assault. The battle raged like an arm-wrestling match, fought with mental energy. Advantage shifted back and forth, enormous force, all in total silence. Jax had tried, and failed, to bend the old man many times throughout the course of their training together. According to Braintree himself, Jax's gift was the greater one by far. The only difference between them was experience. But in the past weeks working with Quackenbush, Jax had clocked more time in the mesmeric link than many hypnotists spent in a lifetime. The gap in know-how was closing.

Jax bore down, his eyes like a magnifying lens, concentrating all his power into a single white-hot point on his adversary's forehead. He had never before felt himself forcefully penetrating the mind of another. But then again, he had never had a subject resist with such strength and skill.

And then he was in, and the PIP image was growing in his field of vision. It took much longer than usual for it to resolve into a clear picture of himself as the old man saw him. But he had done it. Braintree was his. He knew a moment of triumph. He had been told what a powerful hypnotist he was, yet this was the first time he'd ever succeeded in hypnotizing anyone powerful.

The heady feeling soon deserted him in a wave of guilt. He had outmuscled his mentor and friend — Axel, who had saved his life and his parents', too; Axel, who had put his own affairs on hold in order to go into hiding with the Opuses and train their son. This was some reward for his devotion!

Never mind that. This is for Axel's own good. No way can you let him go into danger alone.

But the old man was right about one thing: Whether this was a trap or not, Evelyn Lolis needed their help. They couldn't abandon her. The Sandman's Guild looked after its own.

"You're about to drive into the Bronx to help Evelyn Lolis," Jax intoned. "It may seem like there's somebody else in the car with you, but don't worry, you're really by yourself." He remembered his mother's words, and added, "Oh, yeah, and you're driving really carefully. Okay, now when I flash the lights, you'll wake up, feeling refreshed and confident about the job you have to do. You'll remember nothing of this conversation. And you won't see me at all." Hard experience at school had taught him that it was easy to make himself invisible. He just had to remember to keep out of Axel's way.

He flicked the light switch off and on quickly, then followed Braintree out to his car. Too late, he remembered that he hadn't left a note for his parents.

With any luck, we'll be back before they get home from their movie.

There was an anxious moment when Braintree began backing out of the driveway before Jax had gotten into the car, but he managed to stuff himself into the backseat just in time.

Of course he didn't wait for you to get in, Jax berated himself. *He doesn't even know you're with him.* He resolved to stay more focused around the hypnotized Braintree. He couldn't control the danger that might be awaiting them in the Bronx. But it would be a tragedy not to get there at all because of a stupid mistake.

Braintree was a very conscientious driver on the hour-and-a-half trip to the Bronx. The old man kept two hands on the wheel, checked his mirrors constantly, and talked to the voice on his GPS. His only other conversation was with the absent Evelyn Lolis.

"Hang in there, Evelyn. I'm coming to get you. I'll be there soon."

As the neat homes and subdivisions of the suburbs morphed into the urban landscape of the Bronx, Jax felt his stomach tightening. He was in hiding, fearing for his life and the lives of his family. Why would he deliberately place himself back in the line of fire in what might very well turn out to be a trap? This was Sentia's city, Mako's city. The closer they got to the corner of Eighty-Ninth and Crummel, the louder the alarm bells rang in his ears.

The streets grew narrower, darker, and apartment buildings gave way to tenements and, finally, old warehouses with broken windows and security gates spray-painted with graffiti. The streets were deserted. Two of every three streetlights were out, so the shadows loomed long and dark on the pavement.

The 1999 Avenger lurched up to the curb and parked behind an ancient pickup truck. Alert, Jax jumped out before Braintree locked the car. He followed his mentor over broken pavement, across the street to where a sign declared: CAISTER & SONS, QUALITY MEATS. The hypnotic command was holding. The old man seemed oblivious to Jax's presence, even though his gaze panned across him several times. It felt odd to be totally ignored by someone who normally had a comment for every occasion.

Hugging the dirty brick of the building, Jax watched as Braintree tried to call Lolis. Her number rang and rang, but there was no answer. Finally, the old man headed into the building. There was a padlock on the heavy steel door, but it was hanging open and seemed to be broken.

The whole thing screamed setup, Jax thought, his hair standing on the back of his neck. He fought the wild impulse to wake Braintree and get the two of them out of there. But what would that solve? Lolis was still missing, and others, too. The key to finding them seemed to lie somewhere in this warehouse.

Boldly, the old man ventured into the gloom of the building, navigating by the light of his cell phone. There were six concrete steps directly ahead, leading up to a set of heavy double doors.

Acting on pure instinct, Jax hung back, keeping well hidden. If this really did turn out to be a trap, the last thing that made any sense was for both of them to be ambushed and caught. The best way he could help Braintree was by acting as his secret backup.

With a sinking heart, he took stock of himself. He hadn't thought to bring a baseball bat, or even a Swiss Army knife. Some backup he was going to be! If worst came to worst, at least he'd be free to call the police. And, as Braintree often reminded him, he was never without one weapon, a formidable one. He was a sandman.

When Braintree opened the double doors, Jax felt a blast of cold air coming down the stairs at him. Braintree slipped inside, and the doors shut automatically behind him.

Jax became aware of two things: (1) The cold was gone, and (2) so was even the faintest hint of any light. Without Braintree's phone, and too far inside the building to catch any glow from the street, he was suddenly enveloped in thick, suffocating blackness. He knew a panic more basic than his fear that this might be a trap. There was no door, there were no stairs, not even a warehouse. He was suspended in intergalactic space, not knowing which way was up.

Calm down! he ordered himself. *You're no use to anybody if you lose it!*

It was distant, but somewhere in the darkness ahead of him there was the sound of a scuffle, and muffled voices.

Axel! He had to reach his mentor. Desperately, he sprang forward. At least, he thought it was forward. He was flying completely blind, and was shocked beyond belief when he stubbed his toe on the bottom step and fell forward up the stairs. The blow to his face stunned him briefly, and he hung there, clutching the cement, willing himself not to scream in pain. If whoever was inside knew he was there, he would be no use to Braintree.

Recovering at last, he crept to the top on hands and knees until he could feel the heavy double doors in front of him. Wide rubber weather stripping lined the bottom, and no light came through the cracks. He could hear the murmur of voices, but it was impossible to make out what anybody was saying.

Reaching up and fumbling against the door, he found the handles, and hoisted himself to his feet. His knees throbbed. They would probably be black and blue tomorrow — if there *was* a tomorrow.

He eased the door open just a crack and peered inside, feeling the frigid air waft across his face. There was some illumination, but not much, like a building left in security mode, operating only every fourth light. The room was huge, a vast refrigerator, hung with large beef carcasses, and smelling of meat and blood. The space was dominated by a long and elaborate conveyor system of hooks designed to carry the carcasses in a long row up to an elevated butchering platform.

A voice rasped, "I asked you a question! Where is Jackson Opus?"

18

The voice was distant, and distorted by echo in the cold, open room. Jax struggled to locate the source of the sound. At last he saw movement on the platform. He squinted through the imperfect light and could just make out four figures standing up there. Three of them wore ski masks; the fourth, their prisoner, was Braintree.

The old man answered with another question. "Where's Evelyn Lolis?"

A cruel laugh. "Did you really expect her to be here waiting for you?"

So there it was. A trap. And they had walked right in the door.

"Answer me, Grandpa! It's a long way to the floor! Where's Jackson Opus!"

"Nowhere you could find him," Braintree snapped back.

Not unless you spot me sneaking in the door, Jax thought, crawling on his belly into the shadows, taking cover behind the control console for the conveyor.

Another voice said, "What are you wasting your time for? Bend him!"

"I can't take the risk that he'll bend *us*! Come on, man! I want an address!"

"Gettysburg," said Braintree.

"Gettysburg?"

"Right," said Braintree. "Now *that* was an address."

The next sound was unmistakable, even at a distance — the smack of fist on flesh. Jax flinched as if he himself had been hit. He had to do something to take the heat off Braintree. And fast.

Heart pounding, he hugged the control console, feeling urgently for the power switch. He found the largest button and, breathing a silent "Oh, please," dared to press it.

A warning Klaxon sounded twice, and then the system clattered into operation. Meat carcasses marched across the floor, and then began to rise toward the butchering platform. Startled shouts rang from above, and flashlight beams cut the gloom. In alarm, Jax reflected that he'd succeeded in taking the attention off his mentor. But in the process, he'd sacrificed something very important. The bad guys now knew that Braintree was not alone. How was he going to reach the old man and get him away from here?

Without thinking — because he never would have done it if he'd thought it over — he took a running start, jumped high, and clamped his arms around a moving beef carcass. The thing was cold, and covered in white, slippery fat, but he hung on for dear life. As it carried him across the factory floor, the carcass also hid him from the probing flashlight beams.

When the hoist began to lift the side of beef up toward the platform, Jax knew he had passed the point of no return. He was thinking now, and none of it was very good. What was he going to do when he got up there?

As the carcass rose, Jax got a close-up view of the frantic action on the platform. The three enemies in ski masks were sweeping the space with their flashlights, searching in vain for the phantom intruder. One of them, the biggest, had an iron grip on Braintree. As Jax heaved into view, the hulk's eyes widened inside the eyeholes, and he blurted, *"Dopus!"*

Jax flinched. There was only one person who called him that — Wilson DeVries, who had made his life miserable at Sentia. Even in this crazy position, he felt an extra stab of fear. Was Mako here, too?

Wilson threw Braintree down to the floor of the platform and picked up a meat gaff, a long pole with a hook-like blade on the end. "I'm going to do Dr. Mako a big favor, right here, right now!" He lunged forward at Jax.

Desperately, Jax dug his fingernails into the fatty meat and twisted his body away from the lethal blade. It dug into the meat barely an inch to the left of Jax's torso.

With a howl of outrage, Wilson retrieved the blade and braced himself for a second attack.

"Wilson —" Jax breathed.

Startled at being identified, Wilson interrupted his motion and made the mistake of staring directly at Jackson Opus.

If there had ever been a time for mesmerism to go quickly, this was it. Jax poured everything he had into his hypnotic gaze. *Hurry up!* The mechanism was taking him across the platform. In another few seconds, he'd be out of range!

Come on!

And there it was, a PIP image from Wilson, faint but unmistakable — Jax on the meat hook.

I've got him!

He blurted out his instructions. "Take the stick and knock your buddies off the platform!"

Obediently, the burly Wilson swung the gaff handle at knee level. His two accomplices toppled off the platform down to the hard floor below. Too late, Jax realized that Braintree was also in the line of fire. The pole struck the old man across both calves, and he tumbled over the side.

Past the platform and starting down, Jax knew he would only get one chance. Maintaining his purchase on the meat with his left arm and gripping hard with his thighs, he shot out his right hand and thrust it inside Braintree's jacket. The old man's weight nearly tore him off the carcass, but he squeezed with every muscle in his body, and somehow managed to hold on. As they descended, Braintree succeeded in turning himself around enough to clamp a fist around a beef rib.

"Nice job, Axel! We did it!"

Braintree looked right through him.

He doesn't see me! He's still bent!

"Axel, snap out of it! *Right now!*"

It was definitely not the best time to rouse a subject and throw him for a loop — hanging off a slimy beef carcass over a cement floor. But if anyone was equipped to handle such a rude awakening, it was the president of the Sandman's Guild. Braintree was fully aware of what had occurred at the meat-packing plant, so the only reality for him to adjust to was the fact that Jax was there.

"How did you follow me?" he demanded as the conveyor chain lowered them to the floor.

Jax dropped Braintree, and then stepped off himself. "I didn't," he explained. "I was with you the whole time."

Braintree understood immediately what that meant. "*You* hypnotized *me*?"

"Can we talk about this later?" Jax's voice was strained. "Those are Sentia guys back there. Two of them are probably out of commission, but Wilson won't stay bent for long. Let's just get out of here, okay?"

They burst through the heavy double doors, scrambled down the cement stairs, and made it out to the street. Jax started for the Avenger, but Braintree's attention was on the pickup.

"Do you think this is their car?"

Jax shrugged. "Probably. It's the only one on the block besides yours."

The old man pulled out a pocketknife, and methodically slashed all four tires. "We can't risk being followed," he explained as he and Jax climbed into the Dodge with the dented fender.

They squealed away from the curb and, a few twists and turns later, were merging onto the highway. Jax kept his eyes glued to the side mirror, scanning for signs of pursuit. There were none. At last, he collapsed back into his seat, trying to clean his hands on his jeans, which were just as greasy with beef fat.

"I may never eat another hamburger." He turned to face the driver. "Axel, are you mad at me?"

Braintree never took his concentration from the road. "I told you to stay home. And what did you do? The polar opposite of that. After all the sandmen did to keep you safe, you put yourself in danger."

Jax nodded, contrite. "I'm sorry. And I'm sorry we didn't find Evelyn. But what I meant was — you know — are you mad about *how* I was able to do the polar opposite?"

There was no answer, but Jax could see a crooked smile playing at the corner of Braintree's mouth.

"And I did rescue you," Jax dared to add.

"Quit while you're ahead, kid."

Jax turned solemn. "That was Wilson DeVries, and probably a couple of other hypnos from Sentia. I keep wondering why Mako didn't come himself."

"Maybe he doesn't like to get his hands dirty. Or maybe those honor students are working for themselves this time. Or for someone else entirely."

Jax was mystified. "Who else would be after me?"

"Anyone who knows what you can do," the old man replied readily. "How about Avery Quackenbush?"

"He doesn't need to chase me," Jax observed. "I show up on his doorstep five days a week."

"I don't pretend to understand what goes on under the hood of a muck-a-muck like that. But if he tracked you down, there must be others who'll try. You rigged an election, and you're not even thirteen yet. The sky's the limit for what you might be capable of." Braintree let out a long breath and relaxed his grip on the wheel. "Whoever's holding Evelyn and the others, their purpose is to draw *you* out of hiding. And you just came out and waltzed right into their roach motel. Now they know that you're close, and that you can be reached through me. Not smart."

Jax bit his tongue and settled back in his seat for the drive home. Maybe Braintree was right. But when he thought about his mentor at the mercy of Wilson with a meat gaff, he was confident that tonight had all been worth it.

The signature on the painting read *Vincent*. Jax was no expert, but it looked like a genuine van Gogh to him, probably worth tens of millions of dollars. Avery Quackenbush wasn't the type to put fake art on his walls.

Jax had been left in a waiting room several times at the mansion, and it was never the same one twice. Maybe Zachary was giving him the grand tour one day at a time. If he was trying to impress Jax with his employer's wealth, it was unnecessary for the kid who had already spent so many hours inside the billionaire's head.

Four days had passed since he and Braintree had gone into battle in the meat-packing plant, but the repercussions were still being felt. Yesterday, Jax's clothes from that night had come up in the laundry. Mom was not accepting the excuse that the stains were the result of a science experiment at school.

"But this looks like *blood*!" she'd protested.

"We're doing a unit on dissection."

"What did you dissect — a hippopotamus?"

They'd had the good fortune to make it home from the Bronx before the Opuses' movie let out, but there was no explaining the beef odor and fat residue that a person got from riding a carcass around a giant refrigerated warehouse.

"And *you*!" She had turned on Braintree. "That jacket you took to the dry cleaner. It smelled the same way. You're supposed to be helping Jax, not getting him into trouble."

"I advise him on hypnotic matters; I'm not his parent."

The retort had been surprisingly sharp. Normally, the old man was infinitely patient with Mrs. Opus's nagging. He smiled and nodded through her complaints regarding his personal habits, and tried to ignore her dire warnings about his driving. Lately, though, things had been a little tense. Mom wasn't any different. The big change had been inside Braintree. Saturday night confirmed his worst fears about his sandmen. They weren't just being flaky; they were being kidnapped. And whether Mako was behind it or not, there was no question that the purpose was to find a way to get to Jax.

It was a terrible dilemma. How could he stay on the sidelines in Connecticut while his people were under attack? Yet how could he abandon Jax, and take the risk of that much mesmeric potential falling into the wrong hands? In his efforts to stay on top of both situations, he was driving himself crazy. He had more throwaway phones than pockets, and spent all day keeping tabs on every sandman he could think of. The problem was every time someone didn't pick up for a few hours, he assumed the worst and freaked out all over again. To make matters worse, the estimate for his car repair came in at over three thousand dollars. It was more than he could afford, but he was unwilling to use hypnotism to secure himself a better deal. After all, that was what the Sandman's Guild was all about — living an honest life without cutting corners.

Jax stood up as Dr. Finnerty came into the room.

"Sorry to keep you waiting. Mr. Quackenbush will be ready in a moment."

"Thanks." Jax had been rehearsing his speech all day at school, but his lines deserted him and he blurted, "I was wondering if it would be okay if I . . . I really want to quit this."

The doctor looked surprised, but said nothing, so Jax continued. "My parents are worried about me. My mom says I look awful, and I have no free time to myself. It would be okay if Mr. Quackenbush was getting better. But that's not happening. Is it?"

The doctor shook his head gravely. "He's becoming weaker by the day. Of course, no one ever expected you to *cure* him, merely to prolong his life until the treatment is ready. However, that doesn't seem to be the case either." He hesitated. "Still . . ."

"Still . . . ?" Jax waited for the other shoe to drop.

"I can't put my finger on it, exactly. My *medical* opinion is that he's failing. But my own eyes tell me that the only thing keeping him alive is the hope that you bring him. I know it's not logical, but I believe it to be true."

Jax bit his lip. How could he drop out now?

"I'm not angry that you put your cell phone through the wash, Tuck! I'm angry that you didn't tell me!"

Late that night, the paper-thin walls of the little house rang with Braintree's strident voice. Gone was the affable, soft-spoken little man Jax had first encountered in a New York pizza parlor around the corner from the Sentia Institute. The crisis of disappearing sandmen had amped the guild's founder up to fever pitch. Jax barely recognized his mentor anymore.

Next came the warning knocks against the ceiling. Mom. Now that Braintree was keeping tabs on his group at all hours, she kept the broom right next to her bed.

"No, I'm not your parole officer!" These days, the old man had no volume control. "Our people are getting kidnapped! If I can't reach you, I have to assume you're the latest victim!"

Jax lay in bed, staring at the ceiling. Considering his exhaustion level, he was finding it harder and harder to fall asleep. He could not seem to shut off his racing mind, which was overloaded with an extra ninety-six years of memories from Quackenbush. His own recent experiences had been just as turbulent, if not more. His family was in danger. He was in hiding, pretending to be someone else, living a lie. People who had helped them were being abducted in an effort to smoke him out. And what was his line of defense against this threat? A power that had gotten his ancestors arrested, committed to lunatic asylums, and hanged for treason. A power he didn't understand and was largely afraid to use.

The one person who could help him was falling apart at the seams. Jax never would have believed that mellow oddball Axel could become so nervous, distracted, and ineffective. And right when Jax needed him most. The hypnotic sessions to slow Quackenbush's decline were falling short. If anyone might be able to figure out what to do, it would be Braintree.

The founder of the Sandman's Guild shook his head sadly. "There's nothing more for me to teach you. I can't help you do this thing."

"Of course you can!" Jax urged. "You know more about hypnotism than anyone alive — except maybe Mako. And I'm sure not going to ask *him*."

Braintree had never looked older and more tired. "You've surpassed me. When you bent me last weekend —"

"I shouldn't have done it!" Jax interjected quickly.

"It's the natural order of things. The student eventually becomes the teacher. You were always destined to reach a level of mesmerism beyond my comprehension."

"But I don't want that!" Jax exclaimed.

Braintree was adamant. "It was written in your DNA."

With a tired sigh, Jax got out of bed and opened his laptop. If Braintree couldn't continue his hypnotic education, he would have to get it on his own.

He tried searching for the name *Opus*, but could find no mind-benders in the endless pages of links churned up by Google. The keyword *Sparks* was even less successful. That yielded a steak house, a woman's basketball team, a city in Nevada, and a barbershop quartet. No hypnotists.

It wasn't surprising. Mind-benders often affected the course of history, but they usually did it from the background, pulling strings in their own quiet way. They preferred to influence the big players rather than becoming big players themselves. After all, most mesmeric connections ended with the command "You will remember nothing of this. . . ." It was in this manner that Frederick Opus had convinced Alexander Graham Bell to abandon his dream of an electric fondue pot and concentrate on inventing the telephone. There was no Frederick Opus anywhere on Google, but Bell's name generated thirteen million hits.

Next Jax tried the keyword *hypnotism*, which brought on a landslide of responses. He began to sift through the sites, his brow darkening in frustration. *Quit smoking today! Miracle hypnotic cure!* blazoned one. Another promised: *Overcome your fear of flying through hypnosis!* Jax was disgusted. These weren't real mind-benders; they were phonies, claiming the ability to fix everything short of a rainy day. Weight gain, asthma, forgetfulness, dry mouth, shyness, any kind of mental block. *Are you obsessed with Justin Bieber? Dr. So-and-So can help!*

There were web pages for stage hypnotists who could be hired to perform at weddings and bar mitzvahs, and biographical sites dedicated to Franz Mesmer, Rasputin, and Svengali — a fictional character who hypnotized an ordinary girl into becoming an opera star. This would be impossible in real life, of course. A mind-bender might make a woman sing, but could never give her talent she didn't already have.

He was about to give up when he stumbled on a site with the warning *POSERS AND QUACKS NEED NOT APPLY!!!*

Oh, sure, Jax thought dubiously. *Paper-train your puppy through Hypnosis Dot-Com.* He was about to browse away when the Web address caught his attention for a site marked *Benders Only.*

He frowned. Only real hypnotists called themselves mind-benders. None of the pretenders even knew the term.

He clicked on the link.

20

BENDERS ONLY

The Web's #1 Social Network for Hypnotists, Mesmerists, Mind-Benders, Dream Weavers, Sandmen, and Cortico-Gymnasts

Wide-eyed, Jax scanned his computer screen. Could this possibly be the real thing? Hypnotists were normally so secretive. Yet Benders Only was right out there on the Internet where anybody could see it!

It had to be a scam — the kind of thing Braintree's sandmen were famous for. Jax searched diligently, but couldn't find any trace of a money-making scheme. There was no place that asked for a credit-card number, no address to send a check to, no form to enter personal information. Instead, there were articles that could only have come from genuine mind-benders. "Post-Hypnotic Suggestions That Really Work" . . . "Reaching the Difficult Subject" . . . "I See the PIP; Now What?" . . . "Hypno-Ethics and You." There was a calendar of events, listing meetings in places like San Francisco and

Brisbane, Australia. There was even an advice column, *Ask Penelope*.

ASK PENELOPE

Dear Penelope,

My non-hypnotic son, Aiden, still sucks his thumb at age eleven, and I'm considering a little suggestion to put a stop to it. My husband says this is overstepping, but it's heartbreaking to see the other children teasing Aiden. What should I do?

Torn

Dear Torn,

I know it must seem like a small step to help your son through a painful stage, but using your gift to interfere in people's lives is a slippery slope. One minute it's thumb-sucking; the next, you're choosing his wife. Butt out.

P

Jax scrolled down the page.

Dear Penelope,

I know it's wrong to bend my math teacher into raising my grade, but we're talking about Harvard here. Help!

Seriously Thinking About It

Dear S.T.A.I.,

Studying, not scheming, will get you into the Ivy League. Buckle down and hit the books!

P

Dear Penelope,

My boyfriend wants me to try blue-colored contact lenses, but I'm afraid they'll block my mesmeric ability, which is the only way I can get him to put the toilet seat down. Am I being a Nervous Nellie here?

Brown-Eyed in Boise

Dear Brown-Eyed,

You're not being nervous at all. Anything in front of the irises can affect hypnotic power. From where I sit, the problem is this so-called boyfriend. Trust me, if he can't accept you the way you are, then the toilet seat is just the beginning. Brown is beautiful! Dump him!

P

Jax was astounded. The hypnotists he'd worked with treated their talent like a deep, dark secret. But here, complicated mesmeric procedures and paranormal phenomena were swapped like recipes for homemade brownies. Penelope alone handed out more information than he'd ever received from all the mind-benders he knew combined, except for Braintree. She was practically the Axel of the Internet, dispensing advice and reminding people not to go overboard using their abilities for frivolous purposes or personal gain. Come to think of it, that's what Benders Only reminded him of — a kind of online Sandman's Guild for hypnotists all around the world.

An odd thought occurred to him. If Braintree was unavailable, why not post a question on *Ask Penelope*? He mustn't reveal too much, of course, and he definitely couldn't use his real name. But how could he pass up the chance to help Mr. Quackenbush? The tycoon was ninety-six and declining fast. Who knew how much time he had left?

Feeling a little bit foolish, Jax began to type:

Dear Penelope,

I have been bending a person who is very sick, hoping to relax him to slow down the progress of his disease. Has something like this ever been done before? Do you have any advice for me?

He signed it: Trying to Help

Over the next two days, Jax checked the Benders Only site constantly. At school, he slipped into the library during every class change to hop on a computer. Nothing.

Penelope was definitely on the job. She posted answers to Heartbroken, who was looking for his missing wife, in whom he'd planted a post-hypnotic suggestion to "Leave me alone," and to Bears Fan, who was considering bending the quarterback of the Green Bay Packers. But for Trying to Help — who had a chance to save a life — there was nothing.

"Hey, what's this? Some new kind of Facebook site?"

Jax exited the page with a hammerblow to the ESC key. Peering over his shoulder was Felicity.

"Who's Penelope?" she asked him. "Your girlfriend back home?"

"This is my home," Jax gritted. "You should know that, considering you're always spying on us."

Instead of defending herself, she commented in a concerned tone, "Your uncle seems kind of uptight lately. How many phones does he have?"

He sighed. "I don't have a girlfriend named Penelope. I don't have a girlfriend named anything."

"You're so lucky," she said. "I'm not allowed on Facebook."

He almost bit her head off. "It wasn't Facebook! I'm just . . . surfing, that's all."

"Looking for a dentist who won't make you go every day?"

Jax was grateful when the bell rang. It was the only way to turn her off.

He didn't get another chance to visit Benders Only until after he got home from the Quackenbush mansion. He clicked on *Ask Penelope* and there it was:

Dear Trying to Help,

You didn't provide much detail about your friend's condition, but to increase the intensity of a hypnotic connection, there's a certain technique that has always worked for me. As they say, it's all done with mirrors. Enjoy!

P

Directly below was a link to another part of the Benders Only site. Jax was redirected to an article entitled "Improving Your Craft: Level Six — Boost the Bend." He devoured it with the velocity of a speed-reader. It was written by a Russian hypnotist named Yevgeny Bobrov, who claimed the mesmeric experience could be intensified by bending your subject while the two of you sat between two mirrored walls. The author didn't understand exactly how it worked. But he believed that the endless reflections acted as a mental lens that magnified the hypnotic effect in much the way that an optical lens worked inside a microscope or telescope.

Jax dialed the switchboard operator at the mansion. "I need to talk to Mr. Quackenbush. This is . . ." He hesitated. The tycoon knew his real name, but there was no point advertising it to anybody else. "Jack Magnus."

A few seconds later, Zachary came on the line. "Yes, Mr. Jack, what can I do for you?"

"I know it's late, Zachary, but I need to talk to him. It's urgent."

It seemed an eternity before Jax heard the feeble onionskin voice. "The last person who tried to drag me to the phone at this hour was President Clinton. But I guess I need you more than I ever needed him. What's up, kid?"

"I figured out something to try, but I wanted to make sure it was okay with you."

The billionaire managed a raspy laugh. "Well, so long as it doesn't interfere with my zip-lining and my trampolining, I'll give it a shot."

Jax was worried. "Shouldn't we ask Dr. Finnerty's permission first?"

For a moment, Jax heard the young, confident Avery Quackenbush he had only met in memories.

"*I* give the orders around here. Finnerty does what he's told."

21

It was the same tooled-leather table, but now it was bracketed by two massive mirrors that must have stood twenty feet high, literally scraping the ceiling of the billionaire's sitting room. Both were intricately decorated in the Art Nouveau style, and gleamed with gold leaf.

"Sorry," Mr. Quackenbush apologized briskly. "Zachary couldn't come up with mirrored walls on such short notice, so I had the Metropolitan Museum of Art truck these up. I'm told they used to belong to Emperor Franz Josef of Austria-Hungary."

"They're incredible!" Jax told him.

The tycoon offered as much of a shrug as his prison of tubes and wires allowed. "They're not much use to me where I'm headed. Let's just hope they get the job done."

Jax took his seat opposite his subject. The effect was like a carnival funhouse — the two of them sandwiched between the mirrors, reflections extending to infinity. Jax focused his powerful gaze not only on the tycoon, but on his own image repeated dozens of times over. His eyes were already deepening through a plum violet. And when the PIP appeared, it was dizzying. Not only was the subject looking back at Jax, but also at his own image in perfect Austrian glass replicated in shrinking form until it became the tiniest dot.

"You're very relaxed," Jax heard himself say as he watched his countless mouths form the words. "Your breathing is calm and very steady. Your heartbeat slows. . . ." How was he going to concentrate on the subject when there was so much to distract him — so many multi-sized Jaxes and Averys, so much light and detail? He was fast approaching the very limit of his powers of mesmeric control, and the thought of what might come next scared him.

Suddenly, he was aware of a blast of acceleration inside his head, like a plane speeding up for takeoff. The mirror images blurred, and he rocketed into a roiling maelstrom of white-and-gray static. Jax tried to draw in a breath and instead inhaled ice crystals and paralyzing cold. The blizzard was real.

I'm in another one of Quackenbush's memories.

Wind and snow howled in his ears. Spikes on his boots dug into a world that was tilted at an impossibly steep angle.

I don't understand how I'm still on my feet!

He felt a rope in his gloved hands, and traced it to a sturdy harness around his midsection. He was on a mountain! High up, too, because he was panting in the thin air, struggling to gasp out a single word:

"Oscar!"

He knew it as soon as the name passed his cracked lips. He accessed the information in the billionaire's brain. He was on the Abruzzi Spur of K2, the second-highest mountain in the world. He was climbing it with his brother; their native guides had deserted them in the storm, and something had just gone wrong.

Instinctively, he understood exactly where Oscar had to be — less than two hundred feet away, at the other end of this rope. Follow the rope, and he'd find Oscar. Then they could descend to safety together.

Creating footholds by kicking the front points of his crampons into the thick ice, Jax began to work his way laterally across the spur, wrapping the loose cord over his shoulder as he moved. The fatigue was unlike anything he had ever experienced — the screaming of overextended muscles, the Herculean effort required for the simple task of taking in a breath. Visibility was absolutely zero. The air was practically solid with swirling snow and ice. It would be so easy — pleasant almost — just to give up.

But then Oscar would have no chance.

The rope was becoming heavy around his shoulder as he inched along the rock face. Surely the cord was nearing its end. "Oscar!" he shouted into the wind. The billionaire's voice carried less strength and volume than even the papery ninety-six-year-old version Jax had come to know. The call brought no reply.

At first, it was no more than a grayish shape through the blizzard. But as he crept closer, it became all too clear what he was looking at. The other end of the rope was just a few yards away. The harness lay against a snow cornice, empty.

Oscar was not there.

Panic rose in his throat, and he began to scream, discovering in that awful instant all the volume that had eluded him before. Turbulence surrounded him, and for an instant, he thought that he, too, had suffered a catastrophic fall.

And then a huge fist swung out of nowhere and caught him flush in the jaw. He saw stars, wondering who on K2 could muster such strength at this altitude. But as he reeled and regained his balance, he realized that the mountain was gone. In its place was a huge soccer stadium, draped in British Union Jacks. Fans poured out the exits, sprinting for the parking lot, where an enormous brawl was in progress. Rather than trying to escape the violence, they were running joyfully toward it, eager to take part. And he was right in the middle of everything, trading blows with the best of them.

No! Jax thought desperately. *I can't be here! I'm supposed to be on K2!*

He attempted to concentrate all the power of his hypnotic mind on a return to Pakistan and K2, but a haymaker took him across the side of the head, and fighting off the dizziness required all his attention.

He shook himself back to awareness, ducking a punch that struck a hapless combatant behind him. He had to get out of this session. He wasn't sure if it was the mirrors or not, but he was hopelessly lost in these memories, and needed to ground himself before he was carried even further away from reality.

"When I snap my fingers," he tried to say, "you'll wake up. . . ."

It didn't work. He was still in the fight outside the soccer stadium, wrestling with somebody huge. He dispatched his opponent with a well-placed knee, and made a concerted effort to return to the mansion and the real world: "Wake up, Mr. Quackenbush. We have to talk about this!"

Something was misfiring, because he was pretty sure he never said it out loud.

Another punch rocked him full in the face, and he felt his nose breaking. Through the unimaginable pain, he caught sight of a familiar face at the center of a murderous scuffle by a lamppost. Jax had only seen him before as a child. He was in his late twenties now, but Jax knew instinctively that this was Oscar Quackenbush. Jax watched through his subject's eyes as his younger brother went down under a turmoil of scrambling feet.

He'll be trampled!

With a sense of purpose that lent him superhuman strength, he plowed through the battling crowd and launched himself into the tangle of arms and legs where he'd seen his brother go down. He began pulling off bodies and staring into faces.

"Oscar! *Oscar!*"

Jax barely noticed the blood dribbling down his chin as he hauled the battered fighters from the pile. Where was Oscar?

The last man staggered up off the tarmac. Jax stared. Oscar was nowhere to be found.

Impossible! He was right here! I just saw him!

The soccer stadium receded as the maelstrom encircled him once more. True fear surged inside Jax, and it had nothing to do with any sports brawl or mountaineering accident. He was going to another place — another *memory* — and he had absolutely no idea how to stop it. There was no clear path back to the real world.

The nightmare continued, accelerating in pace. A theater fire, Oscar lost in the chaos. Jax as Avery, hysterical, running up and down the sidewalk, staring into faces as the building burned. Scuba diving in the Caribbean, a passing pod of dolphins turning clear water murky, Oscar's air hose sliced open by a sharp spike of coral. The brothers joyriding on the autobahn in a souped-up Mercedes, Oscar at the wheel, crowing with delight. Jax could see the speedometer needle tipping into unbelievable territory — 270 kilometers per hour . . . *280*. . . .

"Slow down, Oscar! Slow down —"

The vehicle that merged onto the highway in front of them was a Russian-made Lada, its tiny engine laboring to accelerate as the driver shifted gears. Through the billionaire's mind, Jax understood that this was a common hazard on these no-speed-limit roads — the meeting of a high-powered German automobile and a motorized roller skate built somewhere in Eastern Europe.

The gap between the two cars vanished in the blink of an eye.

"Hit the brakes — !" Jax bellowed.

The crash propelled him clear through the windshield,

over the Lada, and across the pavement. The thought registered that he was probably dead, or at least Quackenbush was. At this moment, there didn't seem to be much difference between the two. Gasping, he attempted to pull himself up off the asphalt, and found his hands gripping soft, thick carpeting.

Someone was bending over him. "Are you all right?"

"My brother was driving," Jax mumbled, still half in the memory. "Is he alive?"

Dr. Finnerty's concerned face came slowly into focus. "You fell out of your chair. Actually, it was more like you threw yourself out of it."

It meant only one thing to Jax: *I'm back!* He'd been not at all sure it was going to happen that way.

"How long was I under?" he asked, and held his breath for the answer. It could have been two minutes. It could have been two days.

"Nearly three hours," the doctor replied, helping him to his feet. "I didn't want to disturb you. It was going so well."

"Really?" After what Jax had just been through, he couldn't imagine that the billionaire could be anything but the same trembling wreck that he was.

Finnerty nodded. "I admit I had my doubts. This mirror business still seems very gimmicky. But his vital signs were excellent throughout the whole thing."

Jax looked over at Quackenbush, who was being attended to by his nurses. There was a hint of color in his normally ashen cheeks, and he was sitting upright instead of slumped. "Hey, kid," he called. "Never thought *you'd* be the one they'd have to pick up off the floor."

So the mirrors worked, and Benders Only knew what it was talking about. Jax summoned a smile of resignation. "Mr. Quackenbush, did you ever make it to the top of K2?"

The tycoon laughed. "Ah, so that's what knocked you on your can. No, I never summitted. A freak storm hit high on the mountain and we had to turn back."

"Was that where Oscar got lost?" Jax probed.

Quackenbush looked puzzled. "What are you talking about? Oscar wasn't with me on K2."

At the FBI's Cyber Crime division in Washington, Special Agent Frobisher examined the photograph Agent Lee had just placed on his desk.

"It's just a kid," he said.

"That's consistent with the Vote Whisperer reports," Agent Lee confirmed. "The voice of a young boy."

The Vote Whisperer. Just when it seemed as if the case would go away, someone had dug up this picture — a fair-haired boy, perhaps middle-school age, staring out at the viewer with haunting intensity.

"Some set of peepers on him," Frobisher commented.

"You don't see that every day," Lee agreed. "Of course, they could be purple contact lenses."

"Not sure I'd call that purple. More like phlox, or maybe amethyst." Frobisher frowned. This home renovation was making him color-crazy. He'd started calling yellow lights *saffron*. "You said the clip was all over the Internet. How come we're only finding the picture now?"

"Maybe because of this." She produced a pocket recorder and pressed PLAY.

"In a moment, I will disappear," declared a young voice.

"You will remember nothing of me or this message. Life will continue as usual. But the next time you operate the lever of a voting booth, it will be your overwhelming desire to vote for Trey Douglas."

"The Johns Hopkins professor said it wouldn't work," Frobisher pointed out.

"Well, it did," she countered. "Nobody we showed the clip to had any recollection of seeing it. But when we edited out the command to forget, people remembered just fine."

Her boss took this in. "And Douglas won the election in a landslide." File Twenty-Seven was out of the question now. He was going to have to alert his superiors. There seemed to be something truly sinister going on — not that the boy in the picture seemed like a criminal. Still, election tampering, hypnotic mind control — it was really serious stuff.

He asked the million-dollar question. "Who's the kid?"

"We already ran the picture through the facial-recognition database," she replied. "One hit: Jackson Opus, twelve years old, a seventh grader at I.S. 222 in New York City. His file's been altered, but it's definitely him."

"Well, what are we waiting for?" Frobisher exclaimed, tossing the Vote Whisperer file into his briefcase. "Have the Manhattan field office bring him in. I'll be on the next flight."

"There's a problem," Lee said gravely. "Jackson Opus disappeared months ago. Nobody has seen him or his family since."

Axel Braintree's short legs pumped the pedals of the bike, which tooled along the roadway in New York's Central Park. He hadn't cycled in years, but his daily exercises kept him in top physical shape. And here was the payoff — strength in his body and plenty of wind. He needed his breath in order to run this extraordinary emergency gathering of the Sandman's Guild.

Eighteen of his members had answered the call, buying, renting, and borrowing bikes for this powwow on wheels. No one needed to ask why it had to be a mobile affair. All knew that the guild was in crisis. At least two and possibly more members had been kidnapped, and Braintree himself had been targeted for capture. They were being hunted. It would be far too risky to put so many sandmen under one roof. A conference room could be ambushed or bugged. But no one could bug the great outdoors. And if an attack should come, nineteen people could ride off in nineteen different directions.

They were a motley crew, ranging in age from eighteen to eighty, looking like college kids, homeless people, Wall Streeters, and senior citizens, dressed in everything from sweatpants to suits. Dennison Cho, who was a competitive racer, was glorious in black-and-yellow spandex, riding rings around the others, disappearing up ahead, and then soaring back into view on his ultralight Trek.

Braintree was disgusted. "This isn't the Tour de France, Dennison. We can't have a meeting if one of our members is three quarters of a mile away."

"This is the way I ride," Cho defended himself. "It's not my fault you guys are such slugs. You know, you're not going to build muscle mass unless you feel the burn."

"You want to feel the burn?" panted Tuck, who always wore the robe and rush sandals of a Franciscan friar — not exactly cycle-friendly garb. "How about I set fire to that bumblebee suit of yours?"

"We accomplish nothing if we argue among ourselves," Braintree said sternly, pedaling steadily to keep himself alongside the others. "Evelyn and Ivan are missing. Are there any others I might not be aware of?"

Several names were tossed out — guild members who had not been seen in the last couple of weeks. Three were known to be out of town, a third was under arrest at Rikers Island, awaiting trial for petty larceny. That left two sandmen unaccounted for.

"I knew it." Braintree was visibly agitated. "I could feel it in my sinuses. Four of our people — vanished, probably in hostile hands! How are we going to find them?" He grimaced as Cho took off again, his racing bike barely a whisper and a blur. *"We're not finished yet!"*

Dennison Cho pivoted on his seat and tossed a friendly wave over his shoulder. No way was he going to hold himself back just because the others couldn't keep up. They might have been good sandmen, but athletically, they were all sucking air. Powerful minds; not-so-powerful bodies. Fine, he'd sprint up to the reservoir and swing back in time to catch the end of their conversation.

He was at full speed, the wind whistling through the openings in his helmet, when he noticed a long black SUV keeping pace with him on the main roadway. As he turned to have a look, the big vehicle swerved to cut him off.

His brakes were good, but the action of stopping so suddenly caused the bike to skid out, scraping his left leg painfully against the pavement. Stunned, he lay there, still straddling the Trek.

The rear door of the SUV opened and a tall man with a hawk nose unfolded himself from the backseat.

"Calling the police isn't an option," Braintree was saying as the mobile meeting rolled on. "To them, hypnotism is science fiction. They don't believe anything they can't zip into an evidence bag. Besides, any investigation could lead to Jackson Opus."

"You know, Axel," piped up a young mother who was pulling a baby in a covered infant trailer, "I like Jax, too. And I did my part to help him when he was in trouble. But we need to look after ourselves, too. I mean, I've got my own family to worry about."

"I hear you," Tuck acknowledged with a nod of his tonsure. "We're all in danger now, not just the Opus kid. Don't our lives count as much as his? I'm not saying throw him to the wolves, but what about us?"

Braintree pulled over to the side of the road, and the others gathered around him. "Make no mistake: One day Jackson Opus could very well be the only person alive capable of containing Elias Mako and his ambitions. We need him. The whole world may need him."

A streak of black and yellow screeched to a halt beside them. "What did I miss?"

Tuck shot him a sarcastic glare. "How could we settle anything important without you?"

As the group started up again, Cho maneuvered himself next to Braintree. "I need to talk to you, Axel."

The founder of the guild sighed. "Are you sure you've built enough muscle mass today?"

Cho lowered his voice. "In private."

The two riders hung back until they were bringing up the rear.

"I think I might know where Evelyn and Ivan are," Cho intoned.

"And you're only telling me *now*?" Braintree exploded. "Every minute they're missing, their lives are in greater danger!"

"I — I only just figured it out," Cho stammered.

The old man frowned. "Figured out what?"

"You know — you hear things. People talk. . . . The word on the street . . ."

That was when Braintree noticed that Cho's black-and-yellow spandex wasn't as pristine and perfect as he remembered it. The tight-fitting fabric was torn in a few spots along one leg, revealing glimpses of scraped and bleeding skin.

Still riding slowly at the back of the pack, Braintree peered intently into his companion's eyes. It should have been an easy takedown for such an experienced hypnotist. But he was unable to penetrate his sandman's mind.

There could be only one explanation.

He's already bent — and by someone strong!

"Dennison, listen to me —"

The old man never got to finish the thought. Cho jerked the handlebars, steering his own bike into the rental. The front wheels kissed and Braintree's head slammed against a muscular shoulder. The impact knocked him off the bike — he hit the grass and rolled. Cho jumped the curb and came after him.

"Dennison!"

The cyclist's expression registered zero recognition. He was deeply hypnotized. There was no way to identify the mesmeric mechanism at work inside him, but there seemed very little chance it was anything harmless.

As Cho bore down on him, the old man snatched up a fallen branch and jammed it into the Trek's front wheel. The spokes locked up instantly, and Cho was tossed off the bike. He landed hard on his back and lay there, dazed.

Braintree fought away the impulse to rush to his injured sandman. Cho was bent, and it would be dangerous to engage him when he was under an enemy's power. Besides, that enemy was still around, probably close at hand. The top priority was to warn the others. The old man let fly a piercing two-fingered whistle, the signal to scatter.

A hulking black Cadillac Escalade lurched onto the grass on a direct collision course. The old man leaped back onto his bike and took off. The SUV roared after him, closing the gap in a handful of seconds.

Braintree could feel engine heat emanating from the giant front grill. Were they actually trying to *kill* him? That made no sense. Dead, he'd be useless to them. He was their sole connection to Jax.

His only hope was to find a place where he could fit but the Escalade couldn't. And then he was looking right at it — a wooden footbridge across a gulley, far too narrow for the broad, heavy SUV.

He rattled over the bridge. Behind him, his pursuers pulled up in a spray of turf.

Braintree did not slow down. He cycled through stone gates and was perplexed to see a polar bear regarding him in a bored fashion.

I'm in the Central Park Zoo!

He kept on going, knowing that Fifth Avenue was not far away. If he could make it to the crowded Manhattan streets, it would be easy to melt into the vast city and disappear.

"Hey, you!"

An outraged voice reached him. He turned to see a uniformed zookeeper blocking his way, palm out, cop-style. "You can't bike through the zoo! You need a ticket to be in here!"

"Sorry about that." Braintree hopped down and hypnotized the man with a single dizzying stare. "Listen to me: The temperature is one hundred ten degrees," he said quietly. "You are sweltering in unbearable heat. . . ."

Wilson and DeRon had to jog to keep up with Dr. Mako's long, determined strides.

"I think we're supposed to go in through the front entrance," DeRon panted.

"We're not here to see the penguins," Mako snapped without slowing his pace.

"We'll find him," Wilson promised confidently. "How far could an old geezer get?"

Sentia's director came to an abrupt halt. "This particular old geezer," he said in resignation, "is extremely resourceful."

Wilson and DeRon followed his gaze to the sea-mammal pond. There was a young man in his underwear, sitting amid the otters, pouring cool water over himself with his zookeeper's hat.

Not far away, on Fifth Avenue, an older gentleman dressed in the uniform of the Central Park Zoo climbed into a taxi.

The driver noted his attire. "Hey, you work at the zoo! I used to love going there when I was a kid!"

"It's a mesmerizing place," Axel Braintree agreed.

As the cab made its way through the traffic to the garage where the Avenger was parked, the president of the Sandman's Guild took out his phone and called the eighteen other participants in the day's meeting.

All his sandmen had made it to safety — all but one.

There was no answer from Dennison Cho.

The mirrors stayed up in the sitting room outside Avery Quackenbush's bedchamber. The sessions using the new technique were what Jax's former best friend, Tommy, would have called "über-intense." Jax's involuntary trip through the billionaire's vast museum of experience continued, growing more frightening with each passing day. Most of the recollections were about Oscar — Oscar in trouble, Oscar in danger, Oscar doing something crazy and needing to be bailed out. Judging by what Jax encountered, the tycoon spent half his life feverishly trying to rescue his sibling from every risky situation the younger sibling could get himself into. Avery Quackenbush had been, in every sense of the word, his brother's keeper. And, in some corner of his mind, he still was, even though he was now ancient and Oscar was no longer alive.

The thing was, all these frantic rescue attempts were doomed to failure. As it had played out in the snow cornice on K2 and the pile of brawling fans at the English soccer match, Oscar never seemed to be there to be saved. Avery never reached Oscar as the younger brother was pistol-whipped by Russian border guards. He couldn't find him in the wreckage of the California mudslide that took down two houses. Jax felt the scorching heat of the forest fires that surrounded the tiny hunting lodge. He descended the helicopter's rope ladder to a roof patio that was already partly ablaze.

"Oscar!" he shouted. And up to the pilot. "I have to find my brother!"

"You've got thirty seconds!" came the reply. "If the flames get too close we're all dead!"

The roof felt hot under his feet. When he opened the trapdoor, fire shot out ten feet over his head, scorching his eyebrows. He was too late! The platform trembled and collapsed, dropping him into a house that was already burning. There was no way anyone could survive this.

"Oscar!!" he wailed, looking around desperately. He could see no one — dead or alive — in the inferno. The anguish came then. Jax had experienced it many times before on these journeys, yet that never seemed to prepare him for the next onslaught. Grief and utter failure. A soul-shattering sense of guilt and loss. In his own twelve years, Jax had never known an emotion approaching its power.

I was lucky. When the moment came to save my parents from that subway train, I succeeded. But what if I hadn't? If the unthinkable had happened in that tunnel, is this what I'd have felt?

The last thing Jax remembered before his surroundings blurred and he was slingshot to another place was the bottom rung of the helicopter's rope ladder hitting him in the head. Weeping, he climbed on and hung there, but the forest fire was already gone and he was on a bridge watching his brother go over the side at the end of a bungee cord.

Perhaps even worse than the content of these awful memories was Jax's complete lack of control of his own destiny as he bounced through space and time. Normally, a hypnotist never lost his grounding in reality — whatever might be going on mesmerically, he himself was sitting or standing in a specific spot, running the show. Now he was blowing in the wind, at the mercy of the gusts and currents of ninety-six years of life. Scariest of all, there was no escape hatch or ejection seat. No mechanism for him to disconnect from it all — to disengage from the roller coaster and go back to being Jackson Opus again, even as unsettled as that had become lately. True, it always happened eventually. Some gut-wrenching memory would launch him back to his chair, gasping, trembling, and holding on to the arms, waiting for his racing heart to settle down. But like the rest of it, there was no control. He was a passenger on this wild ride, which meant that the driver's seat was empty. And there was no way of telling where the runaway vehicle would end up.

Nor did the consequences stop when he left the Quackenbush estate. Jax carried the images home with him. They reappeared in his dreams, where they seemed every bit as real as during the sessions. After spending his afternoons trying — and failing — to rescue Oscar, he spent his nights doing exactly the same thing in horrific nightmares. Again and again, he woke up screaming and thrashing in sheets damp with sweat, struggling to reach someone who wasn't there.

His parents pleaded with him to abandon his after-school visits to the Quackenbush estate. "This is affecting you very seriously!" his mother quavered one morning after a particularly violent and restless night. "Have you seen yourself in a mirror lately? You're pale and drawn! You look like a raccoon with black shadows around your eyes!"

"You guys don't understand!" Jax protested.

"Why?" his mother shot back. "Because we're not hypnotists? Because we don't bend minds or whatever hocus-pocus you think you do?"

Jax was impatient. "You know it's real. We wouldn't be here if it wasn't."

"I'm still figuring out the times hypnotism must have been used on me," Mr. Opus added. "Like when I quit that garage band that turned out to be Def Leppard. I wasn't thrilled that my parents used their powers to mess with my life. But I can't remember them ever putting their own health in danger."

Even Braintree got in on the nagging: Jax's health was suffering; his grades were in free fall; he was sleeping for only a few hours a night, rarely more than twenty minutes at a stretch before some terrible dream would cast him awake again.

"Your parents and I have decided that the only solution is to terminate your sessions with Mr. Quackenbush."

"We've been through this already," Jax replied wearily.

"We need the money. If we have to stay hidden forever, it's our only chance at any kind of decent life."

"I don't want money," Monica Opus said stubbornly, "I want my son back."

"Well, as long as you get what *you* want," Jax snapped.

"You've just illustrated our point," Braintree noted. "You're *changing*. The kid I knew would never have talked to his mother that way."

"Sorry," Jax mumbled. "But it isn't just the money. I have a chance to help somebody — maybe save a dying man. How can I just walk away?"

"It's sad that Mr. Quackenbush's health is failing," Dad told him. "But let's face it, Jax. He's ninety-six! Not many people get that kind of time. He has no right to ask for more if it comes at the expense of a twelve-year-old boy with his whole life in front of him."

Jax tried to explain. "The dreams that wake me up at night — they're stressful because I'm trying to rescue my brother —"

Ashton Opus lifted two inches off his chair. "Your *brother*? You don't have a brother!"

"In the dreams, I'm Quackenbush, and *he* has a brother!"

Braintree looked grim. "I warned you that this level of mesmeric connection can have unpredictable side effects."

"Not being able to save somebody — it hurts. A lot." Jax spread his arms. "Don't you see? I have a chance to save Mr. Quackenbush. In real life — not memories or dreams! I have to do this, no matter what happens. I'll never forgive myself if I don't see it through."

The worst part was that Braintree was every bit as against him as Mom and Dad, maybe even more. He blamed Jax for endangering not only his own safety, but also his place in the hypnotic world. To hear Axel tell it, Jax had a responsibility to become some kind of Super-Sandman who would protect the world from unscrupulous mind-benders like Mako.

"You take care of Mako," Jax said shortly. "I'm busy."

"I don't have the ability," Braintree replied honestly. "But you *will*. This horrible thing that is taking over your mind only speaks to how strong your gift is. No ordinary hypnotist could establish a link that borders on the melding of two minds. What we're seeing is nothing less than the great powers of Opus and Sparks coming together. But instead of strengthening you, it's tearing you apart."

The Opuses exchanged horrified glances. The only thing worse than what was happening to their son was the awful reality that *they* had handed it down to him.

"This is partly my fault," Braintree admitted. "Perhaps the fact that your powers have eclipsed mine has tripped my circuit breaker. And I've been distracted by the disappearance of my sandmen. But that's no excuse."

It was too late. Jax was beyond being directed and mentored. His silence said more than a twenty-minute speech. He was determined to stick with Quackenbush until the end. Why couldn't Mom, Dad, and Axel see that? What could be bad about helping somebody the way

Avery had tried again and again to help Oscar? That kind of devotion had to be the purest, most natural thing in the world.

If I had a brother like Oscar, I'd do anything for him.

What could Mom, Dad, and Axel have against that? Was there something they weren't telling him?

What were they hiding?

24

The sea was rough that day, towering waves crashing to the beach, a boiling wall of white water. There was talk on the radio about a big storm stalled offshore. Black clouds could be seen on the horizon, but overhead the sky was clear. A perfect day for surfers. There were quite a few out there, but it was easy to keep an eye on Oscar. He was the hot dog of the group — waving wildly, yelling the loudest, and taking the biggest risks. Watching from the sand, Jax was amazed that he wasn't more worried. Probably because this was Avery's memory, and Avery hadn't been worried that day.

The wipeout was spectacular. All the surfers caught the wave, and the wave caught all of them, flinging them like pick-up sticks. For an instant they were gone beneath the violent sea. Then, one by one, they began bobbing to the surface. Jax did a quick head count. There had been nine. Now there were only eight.

He waited two more heartbeats. Oscar was nowhere to be seen.

Jax hit the sand running. His bare feet were pounding in the surf before he heard the chorus of whistles from the lifeguard chairs.

"Oscar!"

He hurled himself into the surf flailing his arms, desperately feeling for a fallen swimmer in the opaque water. Following his lead, the others began to do the same, combing the sandbar for any sign of the missing Oscar. The lifeguards hit the scene next, plunging in with their rescue float. Jax caught a glimpse of himself in a pair of mirrored sunglasses, and knew instantly that something was wrong.

The reflection was not Avery Quackenbush. It was him — Jackson Opus.

How was that possible in the billionaire's memory?

There was no time to think about that now. "Hurry!" he pleaded. "Before the undertow takes him out!"

Another wave hit, driving Jax under. He forced his eyes open despite the sting of the salt. And there in the murky water, he spied his brother, unconscious and drowning, tossed by the turbulence. With a superhuman effort that physically hurt, he hauled himself upright and Oscar with him.

He threw his arms around his brother, and that was when fate delivered the second shock.

The young teenager he had just pulled out of the ocean was *not* Oscar Quackenbush. . . .

Somehow Jax swallowed the cry of alarm that gathered in his throat. His thumping heart threatened to jump out of his chest as he sat bolt upright in his bed. The pounding in his ears was making him dizzy. He was so stunned that he could not even form the questions that whirled through his mind. Only monosyllables registered: *What? Why? How?*

His life may have been a blizzard of confusion, but until now he had always known what he was seeing: Quackenbush's most intense memories distilled and recycled into Jax's fever dreams. But the events at the beach hadn't come from the tycoon's life. That had been Jax himself reflected in those sunglasses.

His lips formed the final monosyllabic question: *Who?*

That hadn't been Oscar he'd rescued. So who was it?

Suddenly, his own room seemed to be suffocating him. If he didn't get out of here, he was going to start screaming and wake up the whole house again. He staggered into the kitchen as if his knees had locked up, only to find that the air was no more breathable in this part of the house. The back slider beckoned, and before he knew it he was out in the yard, gasping in the chill of the night.

He lay back on a battered lawn recliner, struggling to regain his even respiration. For so long his dreams had consisted exclusively of Quackenbush's memories. Why had that changed? And if the beach scene hadn't come from the billionaire, then what was it? It had started off as a classic saving-Oscar cliff-hanger. But the star had turned out to be Jax himself. And the surfer who'd begun as Oscar? A total stranger.

Or maybe not.

Jax couldn't put his finger on it, but the more he thought about the teenager he'd pulled from the surf, the more familiar the face became.

No! Not possible! You've never laid eyes on that kid!

Strung out as he was, when the bushes rustled, he nearly jumped out of his skin. He sat up with such nervous energy that he managed to fold himself into the chair. There he lay, trapped and struggling, fully expecting to see Elias Mako and half of Sentia storming the property to murder him. Instead, he spied a petite figure clambering over the fence.

Felicity.

For an irrational instant, he reflected that he would have preferred Mako. Then a wave of shame washed over him. Here he was, trussed up like a lobster in a trap in the midst of the worst crisis he'd ever experienced. Of course it had to be Felicity.

"Seems like you could use a little help," she offered.

From the depths of his chair, he said defiantly, "I meant to do this."

Even in his state of agitation, Jax knew he looked like an idiot. But instead of making fun of him, Felicity sprung him from the chair. Whatever else happened, he had to be grateful to her for that.

She sat cross-legged beside him on the grass. "What's wrong? Dentist wearing you out?"

He clenched his jaw and remained silent, determined not to appear any more ridiculous by building on his idiotic fabrication.

If he expected her to mind her own business, he'd picked the wrong girl. "You know, I'm worried about you," she said earnestly.

"I'm fine. I've just been having some weird . . . dreams."

"Me too!" she exclaimed. "Just last night I dreamed I was a turtle. You know what I think it means? I have this hard protective shell on the outside, but deep down I'm really soft." She regarded him expectantly. Obviously, he was now supposed to share something in return.

"I was trying to save this guy who was drowning." Jax had no desire to spill his guts, but he also lacked the strength to make up anything better. "I woke up before I found out what happened to him."

She was intrigued. "Who was it?"

"I don't know." He was surprised at how good it felt to talk about it out loud. He'd been sitting on so much lately that it was building up inside him like steam. Now, at last, he'd found an outlet for some of that trapped pressure. "But here's the thing: I think I'm *supposed* to know."

"Supposed to know?" she echoed.

"It's hard to explain. I never saw him before, but he looks kind of familiar. I guess that doesn't make much sense."

"Maybe it does," she reassured him. "I once read that dreams can be old memories that the waking mind suppresses because they're too painful."

Jax was skeptical. "I think I'd remember it if I pulled some drowning kid out of the ocean."

"It's not the drowning part," she insisted. "It's the kid himself. He's important to you. That's why it seems like you should know him when you don't. What does he look like?"

Jax shrugged. "Pretty normal, I guess. Short, light brown hair, kind of skinny, medium height."

She grinned. "So far you're describing yourself."

He digested this comment. "I suppose so, but I definitely wasn't rescuing myself. I'm not *that* nuts. Yet."

"You're not nuts," she soothed. "But keep thinking about that guy. When you figure out who he is, you'll have the meaning of your dream."

"Maybe I should lift my blinds and leave the light on," Jax suggested sarcastically. "Then if I talk in my sleep, you can read my lips."

Even in the dark, he could see her flush. "Message received. I'll leave you alone. See you at school tomorrow." She headed back over the fence toward home.

She was still watching. He was certain of it. First thing in the morning, she would greet him with: "So, you stayed up till two twenty-seven and nineteen seconds last night. Have you figured out your dream yet?"

That was the kicker. He hadn't been obsessed with the identity of the drowning kid before, but now he was — exhausted and sleepless — thanks to Felicity.

He lay back, staring at the stars. That was another difference between New York and Haywood. You rarely saw any stars over Manhattan because of the lights of the city, but out here a clear night was a planetarium show. He could make out the whole zodiac the way he'd learned it in science. There was the ram — Aries — next to Taurus, the bull. And then the twins — Gemini. He could see only one of them at the time because of a lone puffy cloud obscuring the other brother.

An odd thought occurred to him. The teen from his dream. Similar to Jax, yet a stranger. A brother?

But I don't have a brother!

Felicity's words came back to him: *Dreams are sometimes old memories that the waking mind suppresses because they're too painful.*

That was crazy! He just had brothers on the brain because of Avery and Oscar.

His sessions at the mansion had stirred up so many of the billionaire's memories. What if the effect had backfired, unearthing this long-forgotten brother from the depths of Jax's mind?

Impossible. Don't you think you'd know if you had a brother? Why would Mom and Dad hide something like that from you?

He thought back to the family's decision to leave New York and go into hiding. Come to think of it, the decision to give up their whole lives and careers had been made awfully easily. Had that been done to protect Jax, or to protect this secret: that he had a brother somewhere — a brother he absolutely must not find out about?

This is insane! Mom and Dad would never deceive me like that.

The thought had barely occurred to him when he realized it was 100 percent wrong. For twelve years, Dad had concealed from him the fact that he was descended from a long line of powerful hypnotists. That had to be at least as big as this.

He felt the lawn chair spinning underneath him. If

this was true, everything Jax thought he knew about his life might be a lie. And everyone he thought was on his side could well be an enemy.

He was going to have to start from scratch, to learn what was real and what was not.

25

“Mom,” Jax asked at breakfast the next morning, “how come you and Dad only had one kid?”

“Oh, I don’t know,” she replied, refilling his cereal bowl. “We talked about a bigger family, but I suppose we were selfish. I could blame New York a little for that. We were both so wrapped up in our careers. . . .” Her voice trailed off, a distant expression in her eyes.

The explanation didn’t ring true to Jax, but it wasn’t yet time to confront his parents directly. Until he understood exactly what they were doing to him and why, he didn’t intend to let them know he suspected anything.

Dad echoed Mom’s sentiments when Jax asked him separately — ambitious careers, small apartments, and a wonderful son who seemed to fill their lives. “And I suppose it was in the back of my mind — you know, my family history. I hadn’t even heard about Mom’s ancestors then. The more kids I had, the greater the chance that one of them would end up —”

“Like me?” Jax could not keep the bitterness out of his voice.

“Hey, none of this is your fault. We’d do anything for you. That’s why we’re all here.”

It brought another thought to Jax's mind: This long-lost brother of his — was he a hypnotist, too? He was every bit as Opus and Sparks as Jax. Was that why the family had jettisoned him? And they'd hung on to Jax because his power hadn't shown itself until he was older? He felt the weight of it pressing down on him. All night he'd tossed and turned, praying that he was wrong about this. Yet the more he thought about it, the more the pieces seemed to fall into place.

The one player he wasn't sure of in this drama was Braintree. Where did the founder of the Sandman's Guild fit in? Did he know about the deception, or was he completely in the dark? There was no question that Axel had saved the family, even putting his own life on hold to help them escape Sentia. But where did his loyalty lie — with the Opuses or with Jax? And after all, Braintree knew more about hypnotism than anybody alive, except maybe Mako. Was it possible that there could be another Opus-Sparks mind-bender who had escaped Braintree's notice?

Not likely.

The thought that followed was even scarier: Did Sentia know about this lost Opus? It certainly hadn't taken Mako long to zero in on Jax. Not much in the mesmeric world escaped the director's notice.

The questions kept piling up, with no indication that he would ever find an answer to any of them. It was nothing less than a complete upending of Jax's universe. Day was night; up was down; friend was foe. And the people he thought he knew were actually strangers, most prominent among them, himself.

School might have been the only thing that kept him from going off the deep end. The regular routine of English into math into science into social studies distracted his mind from the endless loop of mystery, anger, and suspicion. Without it, his brain was a computer programmed to calculate pi to the final digit that would never come.

After school, he continued to visit the mansion for his sessions with Quackenbush, which were becoming even more chaotic and unpredictable. Some of this might have been due to the billionaire's health, which had taken a turn for the worse. According to Dr. Finnerty, the relaxed state brought on by the hypnotic experiences between the mirrors had failed to slow the Catastrophic Systemic Shutdown. It may have been good for the patient's mind, but it was no help for his poor, wasted body.

"Is there something I should be doing?" Jax asked anxiously.

The doctor shook his head sadly. "Decline from CSS is more like a stairway then a ramp. A patient will maintain a level of health for some time, and then drop suddenly to the next step. Mr. Quackenbush has just gone through one of these descents. There was nothing anyone could have done to prevent it."

"Just because I'm dying doesn't mean I'm deaf," came a raspy voice from the doorway.

Jax noted that the billionaire was established in a reclining wheelchair, rather than his usual upright one.

"Don't listen to this sad sack," the billionaire said to Jax. "I have new word from my research team that the treatment is ahead of schedule. It'll be ready inside a month."

Jax caught a look from Finnerty. The doctor shook his head almost imperceptibly. The meaning was clear: The patient didn't have a month.

The other main reason the sessions had become unstable was Jax himself. Just as Quackenbush's recollections had seeped into Jax's mind, Jax's tumultuous thoughts had begun to affect their mesmeric connection. The roller-coaster ride was still about Oscar. But half the time now, the face of the younger Quackenbush brother was actually that of the boy in the ocean. As the afternoons blended one into the other, so the details blended in Jax's mind — Avery's brother, Jax's brother. By the end of the week, this boy had a name: Liam. Liam Opus was as real to Jax as Oscar Quackenbush. And as the tycoon's memory continued to paint a picture of Oscar, so did the details fill in about Liam.

He was older, probably about fifteen. Why didn't he live with his parents and brother? There could be only one explanation for that. He was at the place for a young hypnotist at the intersection of the two greatest mesmeric bloodlines in history: the Sentia Institute, learning at the side of Elias Mako himself. Jax was fuzzy on some of the particulars. That was probably because his mind had been sunk so far into Quackenbush's memories that a degree of confusion had to be expected. It was just as Braintree had warned.

For instance, Jax himself had studied at Sentia, but he didn't remember meeting Liam there. Why not? And when Mom and Dad had "rescued" him from Mako, why hadn't they rescued Liam, too? How could parents love one son and not the other?

He was missing something here. But what?

Jax knew he was losing his grip on reality in the swirl of Quackenbush's recollections and his own dreams. His response was to cling to the one thing that seemed most important: Liam. His lost brother was growing by the day, assuming face and form and voice. And as Jax struggled to order his world to include Liam, his mind made the necessary adjustments to the basic building blocks of what he should have known to be true.

For example, Elias Mako was no longer the bad guy. He was the good guy, who had taken in Liam Opus and was developing him as a mind-bender. Jax should have been with them, working side by side with his brother. But his parents had taken him away for their own inscrutable reasons. As non-hypnotists, they had needed mesmeric support in the plot. So they had brought in the Sandman's Guild. Jax should have seen that from the beginning. Braintree was Dr. Mako's sworn enemy, which automatically put him on the wrong side. For all this time, his parents had been complaining about their "exile" in Haywood. And the whole time, the banished one had been Jax.

If the atmosphere in the little house had been tense before, it now vibrated like a guitar string. Jax's communication with his parents had been reduced to a series of grunts. He felt he owed no more to people who were essentially his jailers.

His parents and Braintree continued to stick to their story that all his problems would disappear if only he would give up his daily visits to the Quackenbush mansion. That earned the most dismissive grunt of all. Did they think he was so stupid that he would never figure out how he'd been duped and manipulated?

Dad had taken to working late, and avoiding the house except to eat and sleep. Mom was tackling a six-inch-thick psychology textbook entitled *The Difficult Adolescent Years*. Like that had anything to do with what was going on!

Axel Braintree was slowly coming to realize that Jax's state was every bit as alarming as the disappearance of the sandmen in New York. His hypnotic expertise had warned him to expect some side effects as a result of Jax's prolonged sessions with Quackenbush — uneasy dreams, interrupted sleep, even a tendency to identify with his subject. Yet this went far beyond that. Jax's entire personality had changed. He was hostile. Worse, he had tuned everybody out, so it was impossible to ask him what was making him so angry. It was devastating his parents, who had already suffered a lot because of their devotion to their son. And it presented a practical problem. They were supposed to be hiding out here. How could they impersonate a normal Connecticut family when the entire household was completely melting down?

"You should cut your parents some slack," he advised. "They didn't ask for this any more than you did."

Jax's answer was a surly, mumbled, "I'm late for the bus."

Braintree tried again. "I'll give you a ride."

"I'd rather live." It was just a growl.

As Jax breezed past him, the old man stepped out in front of his protégé and fixed him with his best mesmeric stare. Braintree knew he was no longer as powerful as Jax. But he had to make one last-ditch effort to find out what was going on inside that handsome head.

Caught off guard, Jax was unprepared to defend against the assault. In that instant, the founder of the Sandman's Guild concentrated his considerable ability like a pinpoint laser in an attempt to see and understand as much as he could.

The glimpse was brief, but it left Braintree gasping with shock. He would not have believed there could be so much chaos and confusion boiling around the mind of someone so young. He struggled to find a focal point in the turbulence, yet at that moment, Jax mustered his defenses and cast the intruder out. The force of it left Braintree staggering.

"Don't ever do that again!" Jax ordered, then stormed out of the house.

The old man stood in the foyer, panting with exertion, trying to make sense of what he had seen. He knew as much about hypnotism as anyone alive, but nothing could have prepared him for the firestorm he'd encountered inside Jax's head. No wonder the poor kid was so messed up. God only knew what it would take to restore his brain to normal — or if it could even be done after so much damage.

He shuddered at the memory of the swirling turmoil. Out of the churning upheaval, a lone figure emerged. A young brown-haired teenager, not much older than Jax himself. Braintree did not recognize the boy. Still, it was clear that this person was a major force in Jax's life. A name began to emerge: Liam.

Who was Liam?

Of the many photographs on the bulletin board, only one drew the attention of everyone who walked into Special Agent Gil Frobisher's office. It was the screenshot of the boy called the Vote Whisperer. The intensity of the gaze and the deep purple eyes made it almost impossible to look away. Frobisher had made the case his top priority, if for no other reason than to get the haunting picture off his wall. It felt like an alien presence in the room. He'd even caught himself talking to it a few times.

"Who are you, Jackson Opus, and what is this strange power you seem to have?"

That question loomed so much larger than the alleged cyber crime the FBI was investigating. It wasn't just that this boy had tried to influence an election, but the seemingly supernatural way he'd gone about it. Telling people to vote for Trey Douglas was one thing. The fact that they all went out and did it was quite another. The first was just advertising; the second was spooky.

"How did you disappear off the face of the earth?"

"He didn't disappear," came Wendy Lee's voice from the doorway. "He moved to Connecticut."

With effort, Frobisher tore his eyes from the screenshot and regarded his partner. "What are you saying?"

"He's living under the alias Jack Magnus, and he's a student at Haywood Middle School. The family's new in town; there's no record of where they came from, or even proof they existed before they got there." She slapped a murky printout onto his desk. "Here's his yearbook photo. Same kid, right?"

Frobisher frowned. "Who wears sunglasses in a school picture?"

"If you were trying to disappear, wouldn't you cover those eyes? It's him, Gil. Facial-recognition software says eighty-seven-percent probability."

Frobisher was already on the phone. "Get me the field office nearest to Haywood, Connecticut. We've got the Vote Whisperer!"

Jax was surprised when he and Zachary were met at the door of the mansion by Dr. Finnerty.

"I'm afraid this has been a wasted trip for you," he told Jax. "My patient isn't well enough to participate today."

"Will he be okay?" Jax asked in concern.

"Of course I'll be okay." The billionaire's wheelchair appeared in the doorway. "Push that sawbones out of the way, and let's get started."

"I don't recommend it, Mr. Quackenbush," the doctor said seriously. "Your vital signs are very weak."

"I'm not dying until I'm good and ready," the tycoon retorted, his voice both weak and belligerent at the same time. "I've got a vital sign for you: Exit."

Jax spoke up. "It's okay, Mr. Quackenbush. We can try again tomorrow."

"Now!"

Everybody jumped to make it so. Ill as he was, Avery Quackenbush could still take command if he had to.

Sandwiched between the mirrors, Jax established the familiar mesmeric link with the billionaire. Almost immediately, he could see what Dr. Finnerty was talking about.

The PIP was feeble at first, and it took much longer to reach the point where Jax was immersed in the old man's mind. Even when the imagery surrounded Jax completely, the colors seemed pale and washed out, almost like old photographs that had begun to fade. A broad, flat expanse with a slightly rippled texture.

Waves?

He stood at the edge of a lake, watching two small boats being rowed up and down, each towing three heavy ropes. The craft were moving in a slow, methodical pattern, covering every inch of the body of water.

Jax shivered and realized that his clothes were damp. A heavy blanket was thrown over his shoulders. He was a teenager again. A slender arm stole around him and pulled him close. He recognized Quackenbush's mother. Yet there was no affection in her embrace. She was stiff and trembling, holding on to him for support and comfort. Jax noticed that he — Avery — was just as tense.

With a shiver of recognition, Jax realized where they were. It was the lake where the two teenage brothers had gone fishing during the Great Depression, hoping to surprise their mother with a fresh trout, a windfall for their sparse table. For all his weeks of travels along the highways and byways of the billionaire's memories, this was the first time he'd ever returned to a single location. Remembering the tycoon's description of that afternoon, Jax wondered where Oscar was right then. *When I heaved him back into the boat,* Quackenbush had recalled the incident, *damned if he didn't have that trout clutched in his arms like a football. We had a real feed that night, let me tell you!*

There was a commotion on one of the boats. The occupants suddenly began hauling on one of the towropes, pulling hard as if they had hooked something heavy. As they worked, Jax realized for the first time that the men were uniformed police officers. They labored, pulling hand over hand, until a long, limp form broke the surface and was hoisted over the gunwale into the craft.

Jax was bewildered by the object's size until he identified what it was. Two arms, two legs — a drowned body. A lifeless white face came into view. Jax stared. It was Liam, cold and dead.

He was aware of how impossible this was — Quackenbush knew nothing of Liam, and Liam could not possibly have been alive during the Great Depression. By this time, Jax's obsession with his long-lost brother had seeped into every corner of his mind, even spilling into his hypnotic sessions with the billionaire. In spite of this understanding, Jax was struck by a wave of grief that almost flattened him.

And then Liam's features began to change. The lifeless eyes grew paler, the lips fuller. Jax watched in amazement as the transformation took place.

It was not Liam at all. It had never been Liam.

It was Oscar.

A gasp escaped Mrs. Quackenbush, and she began to weep softly. Jax felt his diaphragm rising, his body racked with sobs. At that moment, he recognized that the devastating grief was not his own, but Avery's. The family reduced to poverty by the depression; the man of the house who-knew-where, wandering the country in search of work; and added on to that burden, the ultimate loss.

The truth was stunning. Oscar hadn't made it out of the lake that day with a fish in his arms. He had died then and there — as a teenager — despite his brother's best efforts to save him. And that meant he was never in the soccer riot, or the burning cabin, or driving too fast on the autobahn, or in any of the dozens of scenarios Jax had been parachuted into during their mesmeric sessions. The tycoon's mind had created all those moments because of his overpowering guilt at not being able to rescue his younger brother. Jax felt that guilt now — it pressed on him like a twenty-ton weight. It was all he could do to keep from hurling himself into the lake, to share Oscar's fate. Avery Quackenbush had gone on to spectacular success, wealth, and experience denied to all but a few people. And in some remote corner of his mind, he had brought his brother along for the entire ride. In each place, he had attempted to create the rescue he'd failed to complete on this day in the Great Depression. He'd lived nearly a century, achieving virtually everything within the realm of possibility for a human being. This was the one accomplishment that had always escaped him.

Jax felt a surge of sympathy for the tycoon that he never would have believed possible. Quackenbush had countless billions, worldwide fame, a gigantic estate complete with servants, and a private medical research team working on a treatment just for him. None of it had relieved the burden he had carried for eighty long years. Even today he still wasn't free of it. A very real part of him had perished alongside his brother in these cold, dark waters.

And then, at this moment of total clarity, the scene around Jax shattered, the lake disintegrating into a million tiny shards. It was an explosion of spectacular violence, yet it took place in complete silence. Whatever form and color remained began to fade until the world was bleached clean. Jax was —

He was —

Where?

He was no longer teenage Avery; he was himself again, suspended amid a featureless landscape, watching the light fail all around him. He knew a moment of uncertainty. These sessions had taken him to many unfamiliar locations, but they had always been real places, with 360-degree scenery and solid ground under his feet. But this was nowhere; he might as well have been floating through deep space.

He was able to move, although he wasn't quite sure how he was making it happen. It definitely wasn't walking; it felt a little like swimming, but his arms and legs were immobile. Propelled by pure thought, he navigated a tangle of tunnels, desperately searching for a way out.

What's going on?

The past weeks had prepared him for the unexpected, but even the unexpected had always resembled reality.

This was something much, much weirder. It wasn't even *something*; it was more like utter emptiness. Whatever it was, he was trapped in it.

Panic rose from his belly up into his throat. He tried to call for help, but no sound came out. It wasn't a failure of his voice. Sound didn't exist here. Nothing did — only Jax and these endless tunnels. Time itself seemed to stand still. How long had he been wandering? And how long would he wander? There could be no answer. He was lost in every sense of the word. Lost in space. Lost in time. It was as if he had ceased to exist.

Just as he was about to surrender to this limbo, he spied a distant figure at the end of a long foggy corridor. In desperation, he made for it, although how he was moving he could not quite understand. But it was working. He was making progress, his destination growing larger like the proverbial light at the end of the tunnel. He fixed his eyes on it, and tried to focus all his concentration on getting there.

Profound shock: The person was himself, seated at the antique table in the billionaire's bedroom suite.

This isn't the way out! It's just a mirage!

He tried to back away, but apparently his motor mechanism had no reverse. Either that or the figure was holding him here, fixed like a fly in amber.

He was close enough to see his own irises darkening through blue into amethyst, confirming that he was in a deep mesmeric connection. Perhaps this was what Quackenbush saw during their sessions.

Or what I saw reflected back and forth in those mirrors.

The solution that fought its way up through the layers of Jax's confusion was amazingly simple. He had hypnotized his way into this; he had to hypnotize his way out.

He locked his eyes on his image and summoned every ounce of mesmeric strength he could muster. He had no idea if it was even possible to bend your own reflection — if, in fact, this *was* a reflection. For all he knew, the figure was the real Jax, and *he* was the illusion. In this un-place, anything was possible.

He blinked back his doubts and doubled the intensity of his gaze. This would work; it *had* to work. He gritted his teeth, clenching so hard that his jaw began to ache. Where was the PIP? There was no question in his mind that, if he failed here, he would be stranded forever.

An enormous burst of acceleration took hold of him, flinging him forward at dizzying speed. The blackness of the void was replaced by a blizzard of light and color. He braced himself for a devastating collision.

It didn't come.

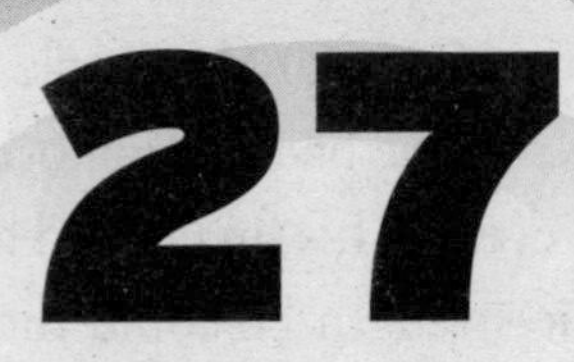

Axel Braintree made it a point to do one hundred deep knee bends every day. It was a routine he'd kept up without fail since his time in prison — a must in his personal exercise regimen.

Until today.

He sat on his small bed in the attic, too upset to worry about his health and deep knee bends. Not even the continuing disappearance of his sandmen was as alarming as what he had glimpsed inside Jax's mind.

It was his fault entirely. He alone had understood the importance of keeping Jax safe from Elias Mako. He had left New York and devoted his life to protecting and training the boy.

How could he have dropped the Frisbee this way? He had allowed himself to become so distracted that he'd barely noticed the disturbed state that was overtaking his pupil. How could he gamble with the mind that might one day wield the greatest mesmeric power in history?

And now that he was back on track, he was very much afraid that it might be too late.

He tore off a quick set of ten knee bends, but his heart

wasn't really in it. Downstairs, he could hear Monica Opus heading for the broom closet. Pretty soon she would be knocking on the ceiling. He couldn't even be mad at her, so badly had he failed her son.

The doorbell rang. Muffled conversation followed, the voices of at least two men. One of them spoke the name "Jackson Opus."

Braintree stiffened. No one in Haywood knew that name. It was Jack Magnus who lived here.

Mrs. Opus repeated the letters: "FBI."

He eased the attic door open a crack in order to eavesdrop more efficiently.

". . . your son's involvement in the creation of a computer virus linked to election tampering . . ."

That was enough for Braintree. He was a law-abiding citizen now, but no good could possibly come of this. Jax would never be able to explain the video virus to the FBI's satisfaction. And even if he could, the investigation would expose him to Mako, which was even worse.

There was only one course of action: Jax needed to disappear again. His parents would be able to join him at some point in the future, but Jax had to go *now* — before returning home to be scooped up by these agents.

Braintree had already scouted an exit strategy for just such an emergency. He opened the dormer window and climbed out onto the sloped roof of the small house. That left him only seven feet of slanted shingles to scramble across before he reached the drainpipe. A few seconds later, he'd shinnied down to the driveway. Good thing he'd kept himself in such top physical shape.

The unmarked FBI car was parked behind his Dodge Avenger. He had to drive across the neighbor's lawn to get around it. That was okay, he reflected as he bounced onto the road and roared off. It wouldn't be the first flower bed he'd flattened in his Connecticut driving career.

Jax had told him the location of the Quackenbush mansion, but he wasn't quite sure of the twists and turns of the trip. He had to get this exactly right.

He couldn't fail Jax again. The stakes were too high.

Jax came back to himself on the couch in the sitting room to find Dr. Finnerty bending over him.

"You're awake," the doctor said, his relief evident. "How do you feel?"

"It was the weirdest time yet!" Jax explained urgently. "The connection broke and everything went dark, but it was like I was trapped there." He paused. "How long was I out?"

"Long enough to give me a scare," Finnerty replied honestly. "About an hour after Mr. Quackenbush —" His voice caught in his throat.

Jax sat up. "What?"

And then he knew. Of course he did. He should have known the instant it happened. The broken link; the darkness. He had lost the connection because there had been no one on the other end.

Avery Quackenbush was dead.

Emotion flooded through Jax. He wasn't sure exactly how he felt — just that he felt it a *lot* — to an extraordinary degree. This was no tragedy. The ninety-six-year-old hadn't exactly been cut down in his prime.

Perhaps it was this: Jax had been trying to prolong this man's life — a life that he had virtually shared during their many sessions together.

And he had failed.

He leaped to his feet. "I want to see him!"

"It might not be good for you."

"I don't care," Jax shot back. "I have to see him one last time — to apologize!"

"Apologize?" Finnerty echoed.

"I was supposed to keep him going until the treatment was ready. I should have been able to save him!"

"Nothing could have saved him," the doctor said firmly. "His body just gave out."

"I could have done *something*!" Jax was babbling now. "I could have planted a hypnotic suggestion that his treatment was ready ahead of time and he was going to be just fine! At least he could have died happy!"

"You're a very kind person," Finnerty told Jax, "but your work here is finished. You did a good job. He liked you."

Jax shook his head. "He didn't like anybody. Except his brother, and *he* died eighty years ago."

"Come and say your good-byes, then," the doctor invited soothingly. "After that, I recommend that you put this part of your life behind you."

The billionaire's body had been established in his elaborate canopy bed. Jax blinked. It was the first time he'd ever seen Avery Quackenbush without an obscuring curtain of wires, tubes, and IV poles. Jax had never been in the presence of a dead person before, but if he had to describe it, he would have used the words "not awful." The billionaire seemed relaxed, relieved of all the tension that his last battle had built up. Jax was in a position to understand, since he'd experienced more of that tumultuous life than anyone except the tycoon himself.

Jax spoke directly to the deceased. "You kept Oscar alive by remembering him. And now I'll remember him for you." He backtracked to the door. "Bye, Mr. Quackenbush."

Zachary stepped forward. "I'll give you a ride home now, Mr. Jack."

As the Bentley tooled along the rural roads, Zachary reached over the partition and handed Jax an envelope. "It's a cashier's check for five hundred thousand dollars. Mr. Quackenbush always pays his debts."

Jax pocketed the envelope without even examining the contents. He'd almost forgotten the deal that had convinced him to sign on with Quackenbush in the first place — money to replace the careers his parents had to give up when the Opuses went into hiding. Now he had that money in his hand. What was missing was the family. His parents had betrayed him, keeping him in the dark about Liam, his own flesh-and-blood brother. Worse, they were depriving him of his rightful place — alongside Liam and Dr. Mako — in mesmeric history. The money was supposed to be their future, but he had no future with

Ashton and Monica Opus — and not with Axel Braintree either. For everything Braintree had taught him about hypnotism, he had passed on at least ten lies. Sentia was not the enemy; the enemy was living under the very same roof as Jax himself.

In that instant, Jax knew exactly what he had to do. Why should he return home to that place that was not home? To go through the motions and continue that sham of a life? No, he had already wasted enough time in ignorance. It was time to start building the real Jackson Opus. And he would do it with his brother at his side — at Sentia, where they both belonged, learning from the great Dr. Mako.

"Is it okay if you drop me off in town instead of at my house?" Jax requested. "I want to go to the bank and deposit this check."

"Good idea," Zachary approved. "Mr. Quackenbush always said you had a head on your shoulders." He peered back over the partition with a sad smile. "He didn't say that about everybody, you know."

Jax knew. He also knew that he wasn't going to be making any deposit that day. The bank was located next to the train station. New York was less than two hours away.

Jack Magnus was dead. Long live Jackson Opus.

He was going home.

Spicy food always made Felicity hyper.

That was why she was sitting in the window of El Rancho Pancho with a basket of tortilla chips and their famous habanero salsa. Her parents had her on a strict diet of mild-to-medium. So when they were both working late, El Rancho Pancho was the spot where she could treat herself to something a little more incendiary.

There she sat, her tongue on fire, watching the businesspeople swarm off the commuter trains at the station across the street. At this hour, the open-air platform emptied out quickly. Only one figure was waiting for a train to take him *from* Haywood rather than the other way around. A blob of salsa dripped onto the knee of her jeans. It was Jack Magnus, and he was pacing like he was about to start running down the track, rather than wait for the train.

She tossed some bills onto her table, ran out of the restaurant, and crossed the street to the station.

"Jack! What's up! Where are you going?"

He looked frantic. His face was pale, and his eyes, which never seemed to be the same color twice, were eggplant purple. His hands were shaky, and when he recognized her, he quickly jammed them into his pockets.

"Hi," he said in somebody else's voice.

"You're taking a train *now*?"

He nodded vigorously. "I'm going to New York."

She was mystified. "Is there some big concert tonight?"

He was tight-lipped. "I'm going to find my brother."

"But you're an only child!"

The story that she heard next had her head spinning — and it had nothing to do with the habanero peppers in the salsa. Jack had a secret brother who his parents had been hiding for all these years. Liam lived in some kind of research lab in New York. Jack wasn't too clear on what his brother was doing there. Had Liam been committed to an institution? Maybe, but sometimes it sounded more as if Liam was the privileged son, and Jack had gotten the short end of the stick by being taken to Haywood with his parents and uncle. One thing was obvious: Jack was beyond furious with his family, and upset to the point where he wasn't thinking clearly. His plan, as much as she could decipher it, was to join Liam at this institute, which was a wonderful place, run by a great man named Dr. Mako.

"What kind of institute is it?" Felicity asked, mystified.

"It's . . . brain research."

"You're a seventh grader!" she exploded. "What kind of brain research could you possibly be doing?"

"I can't tell you," he said evasively. "It's something that runs in my family. Liam's got it, and so do I."

The train appeared as a single headlight in the distance. In a minute or two, it would be here. Then Jack would be aboard and gone, on his way to his brother and that institute, whatever it was. She didn't have to think too hard to realize that his story made very little sense. And even if he was telling the truth, it was clear that he was too stressed out to be making huge decisions like running away from home. She had observed Jack becoming increasingly tense and distant in the past weeks — why else would a guy be sitting out in his backyard at two AM? She'd never realized just how far gone he was.

As the train pulled into the station, Felicity understood she had a decision to make. She liked Jack a lot, and if he wasn't quite as friendly in return, it was only because of all the weird stuff he had to contend with. Haywood was so boring, and he was the most interesting thing ever to show up in town. As his friend, she had a responsibility to stick with him at this dangerous time to make sure he didn't mess up his life. With any luck, his brother and this Mako guy would convince him that he was too young to strike out on his own. But if worst came to worst, and he insisted on doing something totally crazy, at least she'd be there to call the cops or the Magnuses or both. Even if he stayed angry at her forever, she'd still have the satisfaction of knowing she'd done the right thing.

The doors slid open and Jack stepped aboard. She was half a step behind him.

He looked at her in confusion.

She smiled. "I'll buy my ticket from the conductor."

Braintree didn't like to drive fast.

Actually, he didn't like to drive at all. But he made excellent time getting to the Quackenbush mansion. The house was impressive, and the grounds of the estate even more so. But this was no sightseeing trip. He had to keep Jax from going home, where he would be snatched up by the FBI.

He approached the impressive bronze portal and rang the bell. He rang again. And knocked.

Nobody came.

Strange. Surely a billionaire had enough staff to man the front door. At last, he tried the latch. To his surprise, it opened. He stepped inside, startling a young maid who was standing in the foyer, weeping into her starched white apron.

"What's wrong?" he asked her in amazement.

She blubbered. "Mr. Quackenbush is — he's —"

Braintree was alarmed. "What are you trying to say? Has he died?"

The tears became a torrent.

"Where is Jack Magnus?"

She looked completely blank.

"The boy who comes here every afternoon!"

A deep voice behind him said, "I'm sorry, I didn't catch your name."

Braintree wheeled to find Zachary walking in the front door. "I'm Jack's uncle," he said briskly, sticking to the cover story, although it hardly mattered anymore. "I've come to take him home."

Zachary was stiff and formal. "Jack is no longer here, and he won't be returning. I'm not at liberty to give out any further information."

The founder of the Sandman's Guild understood that everyone was at liberty to give out information under the right circumstances. He locked eyes with Zachary and had him hypnotized inside of five seconds.

"Now that I have your attention, you will tell me where Jack Magnus is."

"I took him to Haywood," Zachary droned. "To the bank."

"Why the bank?" Braintree probed.

"He had a large check from Mr. Quackenbush."

Braintree knew that Jax had no bank account in Haywood. The Opuses had set up a joint account for themselves, but had not bothered to open one for Jax. It had been their goal to be able to resume their New York lives someday soon.

What could Jax have hoped to accomplish at a bank?

"Think back to when Jack got out of your car," the sandman persisted. "What did he do next?"

"He went to the bank."

"You are reliving this moment second by second. Jack leaves the car and shuts the door. Tell me exactly what happens next."

Zachary's report came in the form of a detailed narrative, delivered in a monotone. "He steps up onto the sidewalk and looks in both directions. He approaches the front door of the branch. . . ."

"Does he go inside?" Braintree prompted.

"No. He crosses the street and starts up the concrete stairs. . . ."

The old man was shocked. Those stairs led to the train station — the New York–bound platform. And if Jax was headed for the city in his confused and angry state — and further agitated by the death of Quackenbush — who could guess what his intentions were?

Braintree concentrated his power, determined to scour this man's mind for every last scrap of information. The PIP image grew to fill his entire field of vision, and thousands of impressions appeared in his head, an overwhelming storyboard of months, possibly years of Zachary's life. He labored to filter the information down to the parts that involved Jax, although the task was nearly impossible. He saw so much, yet it was difficult to focus on smaller parts of the greater whole. Braintree had scant experience with this level of mesmeric connection. In this way, too, his pupil had surpassed him.

He was just about to break the link when a fleeting image reached him by sheer random chance. There was the famous tycoon Avery Quackenbush, looking ancient and infirm in a high-tech wheelchair. An attendant was maneuvering him past Doric pillars to the front entrance of a Manhattan brownstone. There was no mistaking the discreet brass plaque next to the door:

SENTIA

ELIAS MAKO, FOUNDER

Braintree felt icy fingers clutching at his heart. Quackenbush had met with Mako?

The true brilliance of the plan laid itself out in all its fiendish glory. Mako had told the billionaire about Jax's extraordinary hypnotic abilities, knowing that the tycoon had the resources to track down anybody. At the same time, the director must have implanted a series of mesmeric time bombs meant for Quackenbush to pass on to Jax. Now those time bombs had gone off, and Jax was on his way to Sentia.

If Mako had tried to trap his quarry at the mansion, there would have been resistance — not only from the boy's considerable mental arsenal, but also from the billionaire and his staff. Even Elias Mako couldn't count on being able to hypnotize *everybody*. Why risk a battle when there was another way — an ingenious way — to compel Jax to serve himself up on a silver platter?

Braintree ended the connection abruptly, which sent Zachary staggering into the arms of the maid. A second later, the president of the Sandman's Guild was in the Avenger, burning rubber for the main gate.

29

“How do you know your way around so well?” Felicity had to scramble to keep up with Jax’s long strides as he led her through the crowded Grand Central Terminal to the subway tunnels below. “It’s like you lived here your whole life.”

He cast her a sideways glance. “I did, until we moved to Connecticut.” He frowned. “No offense, but why are you here?”

“I’m keeping you company,” she replied with a dazzling smile. “My parents are both working late. I’d be bored stiff at home.”

“The thing is,” Jax tried to explain, “I’m going to find my brother. It’s kind of a big deal for me.”

“I can’t wait to meet him.”

Jax regarded her critically. She genuinely didn’t seem to get it. This was a delicate family moment, and she was a total stranger. Of course, he’d never convince *her* of that. She considered herself his best friend in Connecticut. Which she was, he supposed, because of a sheer lack of competition. She was his *only* friend, except for Mr. Quackenbush, and he was dead now. She probably thought spying on people made you their nearest and dearest.

Besides, she never left him alone in Haywood, so why would he expect it to be any different here?

He weighed his options. He could never talk her into backing off; she was just too stubborn. Of course, he could just leave her flat . . . no, he couldn't. How could he strand her in a big city where she didn't know her way around? He couldn't be that cruel. She was never cruel, just nosy.

That meant bringing her along. It would take a little bit of extra explaining at Sentia, but her presence could do no damage. Anybody in the place could hypnotize her and wipe her memory clean of whatever she shouldn't have seen.

"Okay," he told her. "We're looking for the number six train. And when we get where we're going, you have to let me do all the talking, okay?"

She made a zipping-the-lip motion. "You won't even know I'm there."

Jax wasn't holding his breath for that.

As they rose out of the subway entrance at Sixty-Eighth Street, Jax was aware of an overpowering feeling of déjà vu. Had it really been only a matter of months since he'd been a regular at Sentia? To see these familiar stores and buildings on the walk between the subway and the institute was like re-experiencing a past life. It seemed as distant as Avery Quackenbush's childhood memories of the Great Depression.

He steered her past Corrado's Pizza onto East Sixty-Fifth Street — Sentia's block. The institute headquarters was visible now. The sight of its Doric pillars and winged griffins brought out a haunting sense of unease that he couldn't quite explain. Perhaps it was just nervousness at the prospect of meeting his brother. Would Liam be happy he'd come? Would he even remember he had a younger brother named Jackson? For all Jax knew, his brother's memory might have been wiped clean. Look how much he himself had forgotten.

"Classy place" was Felicity's comment.

He did not reply. Something about the institute struck him dumb.

The two stepped off the elevator at the fifth-floor reception area. There, all up and down the hall, were photographs of a tall hawk-nosed man shaking hands with A-list celebrities, ranging from former presidents to actors to sports heroes. Dr. Mako.

Jax frowned with the sudden understanding that there was something important about those pictures. But his train of thought was interrupted when Felicity pointed to one of them and stage-whispered, "Oh, wow, who's that guy with Justin Timberlake?"

He was about to reply when there was a loud gasp followed by the crash of breaking glass. Jax wheeled. Kira Kendall stood staring at him from the wreckage of the water pitcher she had just dropped.

"Jax?"

"Hi, Kira." He retrieved her name as if from some ancient memory. They were the same age, and had been young hypnos together here at the institute. He struggled to cross-reference that with Liam, who would have been there, too — right?

But before he could continue that train of thought, an impeccably dressed woman with supermodel good looks stepped out of her office to investigate the disturbance.

"What was that —?" Maureen Samuels, assistant director of Sentia, stopped short at the sight of Jax. She rushed over and enfolded him in a loving hug. "Jax, I never thought I'd see you again!"

"I — I —" His Sentia experience was returning to him, and none of it was what he expected it to be. "I didn't think I'd come back here. . . ."

"Aren't you going to ask about Liam?" Felicity prompted.

"Liam?" Miss Samuels repeated.

"My brother," Jax supplied.

A violent force yanked him away from the assistant director, and held him in a choke hold. "Welcome home, Dopus! I'd say I've missed you but, you know, honesty is the best policy!"

"Wilson!" Jax gasped as the burly hypno applied pressure to his neck.

"Let go of him!" Felicity cried.

"And you brought your *girlfriend*!" Wilson crowed. "I *knew* it was worth getting out of bed this morning!"

"Let go!" Felicity reared back and delivered a swift kick to the bony part of Wilson's shin.

The big hypno howled in pain, and released his hold on Jax. Jax made it two steps along the hall before an athletic figure tackled him.

DeRon Marcus grinned down at his face. "Miss me?"

Wilson's meaty hand took hold of Jax's collar and dragged him roughly to his feet. "It was a mistake coming here, Dopus, and I'm glad you made it!" He cocked back a fist.

"Jackson Opus," announced a deep, mellow voice from the doorway to the office suites. "What a pleasant surprise."

Dr. Elias Mako.

"Call off your monsters!" Jax panted.

"They're here for your safety," Mako assured him. "Now, to what do we owe the pleasure of this visit?"

"I came to see Liam!"

Dr. Mako looked confused. "And Liam would be . . . ?"

"My brother," said Jax. "Where is he?"

A slow smile of understanding spread across Mako's darkly fierce features. "Why, he's exactly where I put him — inside your mind."

30

Dr. Mako's private parlor was a room that would not have been out of place in an English gentlemen's club. The furniture was overstuffed, a soft glove leather. A roaring fire blazed in the fireplace. Jax sat wedged between Wilson and DeRon, on a small couch opposite the high wingback chair from which Mako himself held court.

Felicity, wide-eyed, was paired with Kira on a loveseat near Jax. It was clear that she was trying to assess just how much danger they might be in. They weren't being held prisoner exactly, but they didn't seem to be free either. The whole atmosphere was pretty threatening. They were badly outnumbered. What had Jack gotten them into?

"Shortly after you disappeared from our little institute," Mako began, "a dying man came to see me. A very wealthy and powerful man."

"Quackenbush," Jax whispered.

"He was seeking a way to prolong his life through hypnotism," Mako went on. "And his limitless resources enabled him to discover what we do here."

Felicity leaped to her feet. *"Hypnotism?"*

"Quiet your companion, or I will," the director warned.

Felicity sat back down beside Kira and made herself small.

"A man capable of learning our little secret might very well be capable of finding the missing Jackson Opus," Mako continued. "So I told him that you were the best in the business, and let him do the legwork. It turned out very well, wouldn't you agree?"

"I don't understand any of this!" Felicity complained in a small voice. "Where's Liam?"

The director folded his arms and leaned back in his oversize chair. "I think by now even Jackson knows the answer to that question."

Jax's thoughts churned feverishly. His parents and Braintree had warned him of the effects that the Quackenbush sessions were having on him. But only now was he beginning to understand just how confused he had become. The images whirled before him — Oscar drowned; Liam drowning. Oscar in trouble; Liam in trouble. Rescuing Oscar; rescuing Liam.

Oscar Quackenbush, younger brother of Avery, who drowned during the Great Depression . . . Liam Opus . . .

"There *is* no Liam," Jax barely whispered.

The director applauded slowly. "Light dawns on young Master Opus."

"But I'm not crazy!" Jax exploded angrily. "You did that to me!"

"The Benders Only website was particularly clever, I thought," Mako went on. "I was fairly certain you'd stumble on it eventually. Your generation trusts Google to do everything. You used those mirrors, didn't you? Did it ever occur to you that, working between endless reflections of your own image, you were actually hypnotizing yourself? Sometimes it's helpful to have your own institute to research such things."

"And you knew I would invent a whole person?" Jax croaked.

"No," the director admitted. "I suspected that a brain link with ninety-six years of memories would be overwhelming to someone your age. I wasn't sure exactly what the effect would be. My hope was that you might become permanently lost in your subject's mind, never to emerge as an intact personality. But, of course, the actual result was beyond my wildest dreams."

Jax stared at him questioningly.

"That you would waltz in my front door and present yourself to me like a special-delivery package. You see, Jackson, I set out to destroy you. But now I realize that the mind of an Opus *and* a Sparks is far too interesting to throw away. We are going to work together again — whether you like it or not."

Jax leaped to his feet. "I'll never work with you, and you can't make me! I'm just as powerful as you, and getting stronger every day!"

Wilson and DeRon wrestled Jax back to the couch.

"Try that again, Dopus," Wilson threatened, "and they'll be picking up the pieces with a shrimp fork."

"Not necessary, Wilson," Mako said blandly. "There are other ways to persuade our friend. His lovely young lady, for example." He reached over to the fireplace, picked up the poker from the implement stand, and leaned it against the firebricks with its tip in the flames.

Felicity let out a whimper of fear as the iron began to heat up.

By the time Gil Frobisher and Wendy Lee arrived at the Magnus house in Haywood, Jax's parents had given up not a single piece of information about their missing son.

"They're a couple of clams, these two," the Connecticut field agent told Frobisher. "They admit to having a son, but his name isn't Opus, and neither is theirs. They say he's probably at a friend's house, but they won't give us any names so we can track the kid down. Like it's no big deal that a twelve-year-old isn't home from school that let out four hours ago. Some parents, huh?"

"We'll take it from here," Frobisher told the man. He and Lee approached the Opuses, who were sitting on the living-room couch, looking tense and worried. Frobisher noted idly that the fabric of the couch and the color of the carpet clashed unhappily. Orange and green — or was it more like rust and seafoam? He shook himself. He had to get his head out of his renovations. The Vote Whisperer case was *this* close to being solved!

"Listen, officer," Ashton Opus spoke up. "We've been answering questions for hours, and we're really tired. Why don't you admit you've got the wrong people, and leave?"

"Let me ask you a question maybe you haven't heard yet," Frobisher suggested. "Does your son have any connection to mind control or hypnotism?"

The Opuses stared at him in shock and chagrin. What did the FBI know?

Frobisher took out the screenshot of Jax from the Vote Whisperer video. "This is Jackson, isn't it? The picture comes from a computer virus that we've identified as election tampering. I'm sure you know that's a very serious charge."

Jax's parents exchanged a look of desperation. It had been hard enough hiding from Elias Mako and Sentia. But what were they going to do next — go on the run from the FBI and the entire United States government? It was time to come clean. Jax was innocent! He had been blackmailed into recording that video!

Ashton Opus spoke up. "This may sound crazy, but our lives are in danger because of our son's special abilities. If we tell you everything, you have to guarantee you'll protect us."

Frobisher sat forward. "You have my word. Where is Jackson right now?"

"We think he's with Axel Braintree," Mr. Opus confessed.

Lee wrote the name down. "And he is . . . ?"

"A — friend of the family," Mrs. Opus supplied. "He snuck out of the house when the first agents arrived. We believe he went to pick up Jax at the Quackenbush mansion."

Frobisher looked startled. "*Avery* Quackenbush?"

"They were sort of working together," Mr. Opus explained. "It's a long story."

"I don't want to alarm you, but we have word that Avery Quackenbush died this afternoon," said Frobisher.

Jax's father snatched up the phone and dialed Braintree's cell number. It rang three times and went to voice mail. "Axel, have you got Jax with you? Call us as soon as you get this! It's an emergency!"

"Give me the number," ordered Lee. "The wireless carrier can track the phone's GPS. We'll find him."

Several very tense minutes passed before Lee got the report. She turned to the others. "Axel Braintree is heading south on I-95 toward New York City."

31

The poker was yellow-hot now, its tip glowing in the flames. Jax couldn't take his eyes off it. As he stared, the overheated iron served as a focal point as his thoughts fell back into order.

It had been Mako. Of course it had been Mako! Who else could reach out blindly from miles away, using nothing less than a dying billionaire as his instrument? How could Jax ever hope to escape this man?

And now he had surrendered not only himself, but also a hostage — poor Felicity, whose only crime was being a snoop. Somehow he had to get her out of this.

"Man, that poker's heating up great," Wilson remarked with relish.

Jax ignored him, and tried to cast Felicity a comforting look. But the girl was too tense even to turn her head. Instead, his gaze found Kira. He noted how grim and nervous she was. Of all the hypnos at Sentia, Kira had always been the nicest. Surely she couldn't feel proud to be a part of this.

He spoke to her in a whisper. "Can't you see how evil he is? How can you have anything to do with him? He's power-mad."

She seemed torn. "I know he wants power. But only for good things — to end wars and make the world a better place."

"Oh, sure," Jax retorted. "With him sitting on the throne. You want a world like that?"

The door was flung wide, smashing against the wall. Into the parlor scrambled Axel Braintree, pink-faced, disheveled, his ponytail undone.

"I'm taking Jax home!"

Wilson stepped into his path, towering over the president of the Sandman's Guild. "Beat it, old man."

In reply, Braintree turned blazing eyes on the big boy. Wilson barely had time to twist away and throw himself on the carpet to avoid being hypnotized on the spot.

Mako got to his feet and looked down at Braintree. "So you finally have your chance to take me on. You're out of your league, Axel. Go back to your pickpockets and hobos."

"Release my pickpockets and hobos, and I will," Braintree replied bitterly. "You've been kidnapping them."

"Such a great loss to humanity," the director said in mock sincerity.

"They're not perfect," Braintree agreed. "But they're working to be better, one day at a time. Can we say the same about you, Elias? You're the worst backslider of all, and on the greatest scale. If you turned up at one of my meetings, I'd welcome you with open arms, because you need the Sandman's Guild more than any of us."

"How dare you?"

Their eyes locked, and the silent battle was on, an epic

clash of mesmeric force that made the air virtually crackle between them. Everyone watched, transfixed. Two of the greatest living hypnotists engaged in single combat, two powerful minds wrestling for the upper hand.

Braintree was a gifted mind-bender, but Jax knew he was no match for Mako, who combined great ability, wily creativity, and cutthroat ruthlessness. With effort, Jax tore his attention away from the confrontation and focused his eyes on Felicity. Slowly, her head turned, and she faced him. The PIP image came to him swiftly. She was under his control. All he had to do was command her. But how could he, without everybody hearing what he was up to? DeRon was still right beside him on the couch.

All at once, he remembered something important: *She reads lips.*

Without a sound, he mouthed his instructions, careful to form every syllable perfectly.

Slowly and deliberately, she picked the crystal vase up from the side table and brought it down full force over DeRon's head. DeRon dropped like a stone.

"Hey!" Wilson was up, lunging for Jax, but Jax was no longer on the couch. He dropped to the floor, rolled once, and fished the hot poker from the fire. Brandishing it in the *en garde* style, he held it out, keeping Wilson at bay. Jax might have been the scrub of the Haywood Middle School fencing team, but the skills he'd learned were coming in handy.

Ordering Felicity behind him, he grabbed Braintree's arm, pulling him away from the confrontation with Mako.

Both combatants came back to reality with twin roars of protest.

"I was winning!" Braintree complained.

Kira snatched up a hearth broom and tried to whack the poker out of Jax's hand. Deftly, Jax twisted his wrist and thrust forward. The handle lifted from her grip, and the small broom went skittering across the floor. Coach Riley would have been proud.

Under cover of the poker, the three ran out the door and slammed it behind them. Braintree looked up and down the hall, settling on a burly janitor who was mopping the floor. Still geared up from his battle with Mako, he hypnotized the man almost instantaneously and ordered him to the parlor door.

"All the evil in the world is inside this room. Don't let it out! Keep the door shut. Your very life depends on it!"

The man clutched the knob and held on with intense determination.

They fled, Jax in the lead, still holding the poker. He threw open the stairwell doors, and they started down, running full tilt.

"Axel, I was such an idiot —"

"Apologize later!" Braintree cut him off, hair wild. "Right now, our priority is not dying, and that requires speed!"

Felicity stumbled along, trembling and sobbing with every step.

Hoping that some trace of a mesmeric link still existed between them, Jax panted, "You feel calm and relaxed, and you know that everything is going to be all right."

"What are you talking about, Jack Magnus?" she exploded in a fury. "*Nothing* is going to be all right! Weren't you paying attention back there? I can't believe I thought you were interesting! You're not interesting — you're *completely insane*!"

As Jax gestured his innocence, the poker slipped from his hand and clattered past the first-floor landing, all the way to the basement level.

"Leave it!" Braintree puffed. "That janitor won't hold them forever!"

But Jax started down the basement steps. "We might need a weapon." He could see the poker at the bottom of the stairs, the tip still glowing. As he grabbed it, he was already on the way up again.

That was when he heard the sound — a distant tapping.

Who cares? So they've got an old boiler or something! Get out of there!

He listened more closely. There was a rhythm to it.

Boilers don't have rhythm!

"Are you writing an opera down there?" Braintree rasped from above.

"Just a minute," Jax called back. Three quick taps, three slower ones, followed by three more quick ones.

That's SOS *in Morse code!*

"Axel, you'd better come down here."

"Why?"

"I — I think I might have found your sandmen!"

32

Braintree reacted immediately. He turned his eyes on Felicity, established a mesmeric link, and plopped his cell phone in her hand. "You will get out of here — *fast*! Run five blocks in any direction, and call your parents to come and get you. You will remember nothing of what you saw here today. You won't even remember how you got to New York or who you were with. Now, *go*!"

He watched her run out the door, and then dashed down the stairs to join Jax.

"Where's Felicity?" Jax demanded.

"I sent her on with a suggestion," Braintree replied. "She'll call her parents. Now, where are my sandmen?"

"That banging," Jax whispered. "It's *SOS*. Where's it coming from?"

They began to explore the basement, ears alert for any change in the volume of the tapping. A steel door led to the furnace. A room beyond that held hot-water tanks and a trash compacter.

At one point, they seemed so close that Braintree called softly, "Evelyn — Ivan — Dennison —"

But it turned out to be random knocking in the pipes.

"Look!" Jax exclaimed abruptly. There, in the corner of a storage area, what appeared to be a square metal plate lay on the concrete floor. On closer inspection, they could see that a padlock secured a metal hasp at one side. "A trapdoor!" Jax exclaimed.

Braintree dropped to his knees and knocked on the metal cover. "Is anybody there?"

There was a babble of voices, faint but excited.

"Hold on! We're getting you out!" He began to tug at the trapdoor, hoping that the lock would give way. It didn't budge.

"Hurry!" Jax urged.

"I'm a sandman, not a locksmith!"

"Let me try." Jax pressed the hot tip of the poker against the lock mechanism. After a long moment, there was a sizzling sound, followed by an acrid burning smell. The lock opened up and fell away.

Braintree threw open the hatch and peered inside. Five faces stared up at him, the missing sandmen — Evelyn Lolis, Ivan Marcinko, Dennison Cho, and two others. They were pale and dirty, and perhaps a little thinner than he remembered them. But they were alive and well.

One by one, the hostages climbed up out of their sub-basement prison to be welcomed and embraced by their leader.

"I'm so sorry this was done to you!" Braintree told them emotionally. "I'll make it my life's purpose to see that Mako pays for it!"

"Let's just get out of here," said Lolis in an exhausted tone.

They headed back toward the building's exit, but Jax froze at the sound of running feet on the stairs above them. "Too late — they're coming after us. We need to find another way out!"

The group retreated into the furnace room.

"There!" Jax pointed to a narrow rectangular casement window that opened onto a ground-level alley.

They wasted no time. Jax climbed up on a wooden crate and shattered the glass with the poker, clearing away any shards that were left behind. Then he jumped down, and waved the hostages and Braintree ahead of him.

It was a tight squeeze for the bigger sandmen, but soon they were all standing in the alley. At the end of the narrow lane, the bustle of Lexington Avenue beckoned.

"Scatter," ordered Braintree. As his rescued hypnotists ran for freedom, he couldn't resist hissing, *"And don't forget to come to the next meeting!"*

Jax and Braintree brought up the rear. Just before joining the passing parade on the avenue, Jax hid the poker under his jacket. It was no longer burning hot, but he could still sense warmth coming from the tip. "Just in case," he said.

Braintree nodded.

They didn't flee. Instead, they tried to melt into the crowd, strolling along at the speed of the other pedestrians. Jax scanned faces, alert for any Sentia personnel. So far, so good. He risked a glance behind them.

Wilson DeVries was on their tail, walking fast, gaining on them. In a single motion, Jax whipped out the poker, reached down, and sent it spinning along the sidewalk. It struck Wilson at ankle level, taking his feet right out from under him.

Bull's-eye, he thought with satisfaction. His celebration lasted exactly one second. Wilson went down with a yelp and, in the space his broad shoulders vacated, Jax could see another pursuer.

Mako.

The director's dark eyes locked onto Jax and Braintree. He was too far away to be a hypnotic threat, but his expression was terrifying. Someone had dared to defy Elias Mako, and there would be consequences.

As they watched, Mako stuck his head into the open window of a parked Audi. A moment later, the driver climbed out and stood passively on the sidewalk, watching as Mako got behind the wheel. The blue sedan pulled out into traffic.

Braintree and Jax broke into a sprint, but it was obvious that they could never outrun a car. Mako weaved in and out of traffic in a determined attempt to catch up with them.

"He's not the only one who can bend a driver!" Braintree stepped out into the road and attempted to flag down a taxi. The cabbie, however, already had a fare, and veered away before a hypnotic link could be established. Undaunted, the old man peered in the front windshield of a Buick SUV. But that motorist was looking for an address, and had his eyes on the passing buildings, not the sandman in the middle of the avenue.

Jax glanced over his shoulder. Mako was right there. When the light changed, the cars in front of him would move, and he would be upon them. Jax hopped onto the running board of the very next vehicle to come along — a full-size garbage truck, riding low and heavy, with its compactor mechanism locked.

"Hey, mister —" And when the driver looked his way, Jax brought the full power of his Opus and Sparks bloodlines to bear on the hapless sanitation worker. Almost immediately, the PIP showed Jax on the outside of the cab, the Lexington storefronts passing slowly by. "Stop the truck," he ordered. "You have two passengers."

He jumped down, bundled Braintree into the front seat, and climbed in after him. "Okay! Let's roll!"

The truck started again in a grinding of gears.

The wail of sirens cut the air. Jax checked the side mirror. Police cars swarmed around the corner onto Sentia's block.

Jax saw a ray of hope. "We can go to the cops!"

Braintree shook his head. "The FBI was at your house this afternoon. They've traced the video virus to you. No cops."

In the mirror, the blue Audi heaved into view, Mako at the wheel.

"He's right behind us!" Braintree exclaimed nervously.

"Faster!" Jax urged the driver.

The man stepped on the gas. They could feel the

engine revving beneath them, but the truck didn't pick up much speed. At that, there was little room to maneuver on the crowded avenue.

"Dump out the load!" Jax barked suddenly. "Now!"

Obediently, the driver stomped on the brakes and pulled the lever to activate the mechanism. Hemmed in by traffic on both sides, Mako squealed to a halt behind the truck. With a hum of hydraulics, the payload began to rise. Mako could only sit and watch as the compactor door opened and a half ton of refuse came pouring down on the blue car, covering it to the roof.

It would have taken a lot to get a smile out of Jax at that moment, but this succeeded. "That was *awesome*!"

"We're not out of the woods yet," Braintree said grimly. "Keep driving."

But the spectacle of the trash-buried car created a major rubbernecking event. Pedestrians gawked. Drivers got out of their cars for a better view. Workers from a nearby construction site came out to watch. Lexington ground to a near standstill. A symphony of horns sounded. There was even a smattering of applause.

The pile of trash shifted as the door of the Audi was thrust open and Elias Mako emerged, liberally decorated with garbage, crimson with rage. Brushing off all offers of assistance, he stormed over to the construction site and pushed his way through the gate.

Following in the mirror, Jax frowned. "What's he doing?"

Two minutes later, he had his answer. An enormous demolition crane came rumbling up the truck ramp to the street level. As it turned onto the avenue, its caterpillar treads spraying dried clay, Jax spotted Mako standing on the running board, eyes locked on the operator. At the apex of the crane dangled a two-ton wrecking ball, huge, black, and menacing.

By the time the pure lethal malice of Mako's intentions became clear to Jax, it was already too late. The boom of the crane had been maneuvered directly above the garbage truck, the ball looming overhead.

"Get out!" Jax bellowed at the driver.

The sanitation worker slithered out the window of the cab and hit the street running.

There was a strangely quiet click as the mechanism holding the wrecking ball in place let go.

Jax turned to Braintree, his face ghostly white. "Axel —"

There was no time left, not even for last words.

With surprising strength, Braintree pushed Jax down to the floor of the cab, and threw himself on top of him.

Two tons of solid steel dropped from the boom of the crane onto the cab.

Jax knew a devastating impact, followed by darkness.

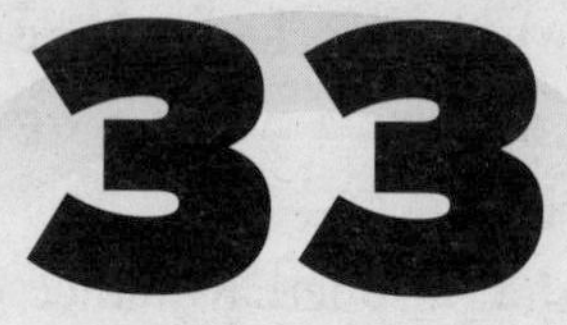

The flash was brilliant, like a supernova. Jax squeezed his eyes shut, but the light reached him anyway. Another burst went off, followed by another — steady staccato flares.

What's going on?

The smell was next.

Garbage?

Then the sounds — voices, traffic, noises of the city.

New York?

He forced his eyelids open and found himself staring directly into the flasher of a parked police cruiser. It all came back to him — Quackenbush's death. Sentia. The kidnapped sandmen. The chase. He was on Lexington Avenue — actually *on* it, sitting on the pavement. The street was cordoned off, and officers were diverting traffic. Trash was everywhere. There was the garbage truck, its cab flattened as if some evil giant had stomped on it.

The wrecking ball!

"Axel?"

Jax leaped to his feet, and was immediately yanked back down again, a sharp pain exploding in his wrist. He was handcuffed to somebody — a tall man in a rumpled suit.

"Easy, son," said Special Agent Frobisher. "You don't want to hurt yourself."

"Where's Axel Braintree?" Jax demanded, looking around frantically. "He was in the truck with me! An old guy with long gray hair!"

"He saved your life," Frobisher said gently.

"Where is he? I have to talk to him!"

The FBI man glanced over to a black NYPD van, where two attendants were placing a body bag into the cargo hold.

"I'm sorry, Jackson. Your friend didn't make it."

The world blurred. Not just from the tears that filled Jax's eyes, but from the crushing mass of his guilt.

Axel wouldn't have come to New York if I hadn't gone to Sentia. This is my fault!

His grief was paralyzing. Braintree had never shown him anything but loyalty, kindness, and support. He had dropped everything to help the Opuses go into hiding. He had stuck with them, even when his sandmen had begun disappearing. He had come to rescue Jax, understanding full well that he'd be putting himself in danger. And, at the last moment, knowing that a two-ton wrecking ball was about to descend on them, he had placed himself between Jax and certain death.

He ran his sleeve over his eyes, and the scene around him came back into focus. There, in the back of a squad car, was an all-too-familiar Roman nose and shock of black hair. It was Mako, in handcuffs.

"*He* did it!" Jax exploded, the poison in his voice

surprising even him. "He killed Axel! I'll testify against him in court! I saw the whole thing!"

"Relax," Frobisher soothed. "NYPD has him. He won't get away with anything."

"Yes, he will!" Jax insisted. "He can hypnotize people and make them do whatever he wants!"

Frobisher cast him a long, searching look. "I've heard that about somebody else." He reached into his suit pocket, took out a piece of paper, and unfolded it. It was the screenshot from the video virus.

For the first time, Jax had a sense that something might be going on beyond the mayhem on the street that had killed his mentor. "Are you a police officer?"

Frobisher flashed his ID. "Special Agent Frobisher, FBI. I investigate cyber crimes. So why don't you tell me about this picture."

Jax's eyes traveled to the police wagon where Braintree's body lay. Axel had always been his guide for situations like this. *He* would have known what to say.

Jax couldn't believe he would never hear that peculiar wisdom again.

"I want to phone my parents."

"You will," Frobisher assured him. "But first I need to know about that video you made."

"Not until I talk to my parents."

The agent pressed harder. "Have you ever heard of election tampering? It's a federal crime, and your face is all over the evidence. You have to explain your side of the story, or you could be my age by the time you get out of prison."

Jax bristled. "Do you think you can *scare* me? Where did you just find me? Under a two-ton wrecking ball dropped by somebody who wanted me dead! And my friend . . ." He was blubbering now, the tears returning in force. "My very good friend *is* dead! I'll — I'll have to live with that! Forever!" He steeled himself and fairly spat the rest. "So take your best shot!"

Frobisher was momentarily silenced by this speech, amazed by the bitterness of Jax's emotions. As he fumbled for his next words, a police lieutenant approached and announced, "Sorry, Frobisher, we have to take the boy."

"What are you talking about?" the FBI man exploded. "He's my suspect! This is a federal investigation!"

The lieutenant shrugged. "This comes straight from the commissioner. The military wants to talk to the kid."

Jax was alarmed. "The military? What does the military want with me?"

"All I know is they flew a brass hat up from the Pentagon just for this."

Frobisher was sullen as he unlocked the handcuffs. "What about my case?"

"Take it up with the army," the lieutenant suggested. "But be careful. They've got bigger guns than we do."

A squad car drove Jax to the Nineteenth Precinct house, where a desk sergeant escorted him down a long corridor into the depths of the building. Passing cops raked him with their eyes. He tried to read their expressions. Was it sympathy? Curiosity? Accusation? In the past few hours, he had lost Avery Quackenbush and Axel Braintree.

In a way, he'd lost Liam, too — not that Liam had ever existed. He'd been captured by Mako, picked up by the FBI, but somehow, that was not enough for one day! No. A final plot twist still awaited him at the end of this hall.

The desk sergeant opened the door and ushered him inside. Standing at the far end of the gray concrete room, wringing their hands with worry, were his parents.

He ran to them, literally threw himself at them. He was so relieved to see them at last that it released all his pent-up emotion.

"Mom, Dad, Axel's dead!"

"We heard, Jax," his father said in a husky voice. "We're so sorry."

"I'm sorry, too! Mako got into my head! He had me thinking all kinds of crazy things, and I blamed you!"

His mother hugged him. "Never mind about that. We're just happy you're safe."

"I don't even know what safe means anymore!" Jax said helplessly. "The FBI knows about me! And what about Sentia? Mako's caught, but what if he bends his way out of it?"

"You don't have to concern yourself with any of that anymore," put in a gruff voice behind them. "As of now, you're in the custody and protection of the United States military."

Jax wheeled to stare at the fourth occupant of the room, a uniformed army officer with a buzz cut, ramrod-straight posture, and the silver eagle of a full colonel on his uniform.

"'Custody and protection'?" Jax repeated. "What's going to happen to us?"

The colonel tried to appear reassuring, which only made him look scarier. "Well, for starters, your life is about to change."

Every time Felicity Green passed the house on Gardenia Street, the FOR RENT sign made her frown.

Why would a family just up and move without so much as a good-bye to anybody? One day, Jack, his parents, and that weird uncle were settled in and making their lives here in Haywood; the next, they were gone without a trace, no forwarding address, nothing. What kind of people would do that? She'd thought she and Jack were good friends.

It had happened on the same day as that spooky experience — when Felicity had woken up in New York with no idea how she'd gotten there. A temporary blackout, their pediatrician had called it. Scary, but there didn't seem to be anything wrong with her. She'd been anxious to tell Jack about it, to see what he thought. But by the time she'd arrived home, the Magnus house was empty.

Too bad. Somehow, she had a feeling he was the kind of person who'd understand.

GORDON KORMAN

is the #1 bestselling author of five books in The 39 Clues series as well as seven books in his Swindle series: *Swindle, Zoobreak, Framed, Showoff, Hideout, Jackpot,* and *Unleashed.* His other books include *This Can't Be Happening at Macdonald Hall!* (published when he was fourteen); *The Toilet Paper Tigers*; the trilogies Island, Everest, Dive, Kidnapped, and Titanic; and the series On the Run. He lives in New York with his family and can be found on the web at www.gordonkorman.com.